A Dirge for St. Monica

Dolores, Volume 3

Hayden Thorne

Published by Hayden Thorne, 2019.

A DIRGE FOR ST. MONICA

*

*

Written by Hayden Thorne

*

Also by Hayden Thorne

Arcana Europa
Guardian Angel
The Flowers of St. Aloysius
Hell-Knights
Children of Hyacinth
The Amaranth Maze
A Murder of Crows

Curiosities
Dollhouse
Automata
Eidolon

Dolores
Ambrose
Echoes in the Glass
A Dirge for St. Monica

Ghosts and Tea
The Ghosts of St. Grimald Priory
Agnes of Haywood Hall

A Most Unearthly Rival
The Haunted Inkwell
The House of Creeping Dolls

Grotesqueries
A Castle for Rowena
The Rusted Lily
Primavera

Masks
Masks: The Original Trilogy
Curse of Arachnaman
Mimi Attacks!
Dr. Morbid's Castle of Blood
The Porcelain Carnival

Standalone
Renfred's Masquerade
Rose and Spindle
Gold in the Clouds
Helleville
Icarus in Flight
Arabesque
Banshee
Wollstone
The Glass Minstrel
Henning
The Twilight Gods
The Book of Lost Princes
The Winter Garden and Other Stories

Desmond and Garrick
The Cecilian Blue-Collar Chronicles

Table of Contents

Chapter 1

Squeaks, clicks, and wheezes—whenever Darcy heard those sounds cutting through the hollow silence of the night, he knew the mothers had arrived for their music. Their lullaby, in truth, and he took a final sip of his hot cocoa before sitting down on the chair he'd moved to the middle of his garret room. A loft, really, but he couldn't help the more romantic (though perhaps untruthful) associations that came with a garret room.

The single bulb dangling from the beam overhead offered him familiar comfort but not as much as his beloved cello, which he expertly cradled with his lower legs. Positioning a large instrument without the aid of an endpin often made him drift into a dreamy, absentminded haze, and he waited for another moment as the mothers inched their way into his world.

Bit by bit, creeping and clawing, dragging themselves by the tips of their bony fingers out of the shadowy corners of the attic room till they rose on unsteady and barely solid legs, the mothers gathered in a small group before Darcy. Some stayed sprawled on their skeletal bellies, some stood swaying a little, and some sat on the floor in hunched and crooked forms.

Skulls in varying degrees of magically stunted decay all turned to face him. Some of the mothers still had hair somehow clinging to their non-existent scalps in earth-caked and brittle clumps. All were dressed in their burial clothes, tattered and faded fabric soiled by two centuries' worth of dirt, with three carrying equally soiled and ruined cloth dolls—heartbreaking reminders of the circumstances surrounding the mothers' deaths.

"I found a piece that's not meant for a cello," Darcy said once his audience had settled down. "But I can still play it for you. I think you'll like it."

He paused and dropped his gaze to the floor, brow wrinkling a little.

"I have a pretty busy week coming up, so if I can't find a new piece to play for you, I hope you won't mind it so much if I used this again," he said in a quieter voice, his mind suddenly flitting elsewhere. To the past again, in truth. "Mom always loved this, anyway. I like to think she's listening to me, too, when you come by for your music." In his head, he couldn't help but add: *This is for you, Mom. I love you.*

He offered the silent women a fond smile and a small nod as he positioned his bow over the strings.

For the next half hour, Darcy played a solo cello arrangement of Mozart's "Eine Kleine Nachtmusik", which would have been an odd choice considering the lighter and more romantic sounds of the original composition, but the mothers loved Darcy's lower pitched cello and the fuller and more resonant sounds it made. No one had complained, anyway. No, not even if the ghosts appeared intact and not in the final stages of decay, when tissue and organ had dried and shriveled, and their presence smelled strongly of earth, rotted wood, and the ever-so-faint stench of human decomposition.

They'd purposefully sought him out in the night, coming to him out of their shadow world, if only to listen to that night's lullaby. They came every seventh night, and Darcy, regardless of his condition, would wait for them and play his cello for an hour, sometimes longer. He'd soothed them in sickness, when his mood was horribly low, and when his day had gone well.

The dead didn't care as long as they got their music.

The entire composition technically ran only around twenty minutes, but Darcy was compelled to start over and keep going two more times after. The mothers didn't want him to stop after the first round, filling the garret with restless clicks and squeaks and stuttering movements as they shifted their weight in a bid to communicate their displeasure at being given less than an hour's worth of music. Not that Darcy minded, anyway, as he found some measure of dark comfort in the company of his nocturnal audience.

Once the hour was up, the mothers withdrew without ceremony.

As a group, they turned around and melted back into the shadows, leaving nothing in their wake but bits of dried soil and the lingering smell of the grave.

Darcy sighed and stood up, gently setting his instrument aside and taking hold of his empty cup.

He abandoned the garret and headed downstairs, the weight of that day's activities finally making itself felt as he yawned and blinked all the way to the tiny kitchen area of the small wood cabin he called his home. He'd have enough hours of sleep, at least, before working.

And with any luck, those bizarre dream-fragments of soft voices calling his name from the deepest shadows wouldn't bother his much-needed rest that night.

* * * *

The chocolate shop was crawling with customers within an hour of its opening. It took another couple of hours or so for the traffic to die down and for the staff—all two of them plus the owner—to finally slow to a more idle and relaxed pace.

"God. Who thought there'd be this much craziness attached to chocolate?" Benjamin asked with a heavy sigh. He rubbed his bald head as was his habit whenever he was exhausted or stressed or baffled. "Thank you, Nana, for your recipes."

"Well—better question would be who thought there'd be this many rich people in Dolores?"

Darcy glanced at Zoe, who was now chugging down her gigantic cup of mocha, which she'd purchased at the coffee shop next door—from the "hot-ass barista" she'd been mooning over since the beginning of time.

"Did you pay for that thing? Or has that creepy flirting thing between you and Joey moved another inch to freebies, finally?" he asked. "And when can the rest of us benefit from your stalking?"

"Joey and Zoe," Benjamin said, chuckling and shaking his head as he went about tidying up the display counter. "It's like a really, really bad romcom."

Zoe merely rolled her eyes at their boss and then glared at Darcy, who was now brandishing the near-empty spray bottle of glass cleaner and a rag as he took his spot on the main floor. The countertop glass display case, sporting too many smudges and handprints, was in dire need of cleaning.

"It hasn't gotten that far yet," she replied eventually. "It did move forward an inch, though. Now he draws a cat next to my name on the cup. See?"

She held up the massive coffee cup, and sure enough, a line drawing of a cat had been made next to Zoe's name, and Darcy was now sure that cup wasn't going to end up in the trash after it was emptied out. Zoe was bound to clean it up and hold on to it for the saints knew how long.

The shop door's bell rang, signaling the appearance of another customer.

"Oh, hey, Darcy—look who's here," Benjamin announced in a voice that sounded far too loud and obvious. "How's it going, guys? Haven't seen you since—oh—two days ago."

Darcy, who stood with his back to the door, colored but didn't let up on his cleaning. Benjamin ought to take care of the newcomers, he told himself.

"It took us two days to finish off your stuff," a voice piped up, equaling Benjamin's chirpy mood, though at least it wasn't raised to near deafening levels.

"Really? That long? I thought it'd be less than a day."

A girl's voice replied, "That's only because Mr. Cocky Hotshot here wouldn't share his stash, and he finished everything himself—took him a couple of days. If it were less than a day, that'd be really disgusting."

"I'd be dead of a heart attack or something. And quit complaining. I gave you a couple of pieces."

"A couple. Yeah, big, fat, hairy deal. Oh, hi, Darcy."

Darcy sighed. It wasn't as though he'd hidden himself from view, was it? He turned to find the newcomers—a young man and a young woman—standing in the middle of the chocolate shop, inexplicably refusing to take a step forward and closer to the counter, where the chocolates were displayed in all their mouth-watering glory. Darcy waved the rag weakly and smiled just as weakly.

"Hi," he said. "How're things coming along in the world of weird things?"

The newcomers—Arlen Stroescu and Gloria de Guzman—looked like a couple of special agents in their all-black ensemble, which included similar tailored jackets. All that was missing was a pair of shades for each as well as hidden futuristic weapons meant for otherworldly threats.

The two worked at the Institute of Arcane Studies (or Arcane Institute) as auxiliary masters who trained up-and-coming sorcerer-hunters and other magic-wielders who dealt with threats from the otherworld. Darcy had always had a massive crush on Arlen, whom he knew was also gay, but who was also married to his job and was hopelessly anal-retentive about sticking to the business at hand whenever he blessed the mortal world with his presence.

There'd been a couple of times before when Darcy, mustering enough courage for an army, greeted Arlen when they happened to be hanging about the same place. In both those times, Arlen had utterly ignored him, his mind clearly fixed on something else very likely more deserving of his time and attention. After two mortifying misses like those, Darcy learned quickly to shut up and vanish in the background.

It was certainly too bad his boss was born sharp—hence his success as a chocolatier—and had read into Darcy's furtive glances correctly. And equally bad was the fact that Benjamin Aaron, genius entrepreneur under thirty who was also formidably armed with his grandmother's secret chocolate recipes, was also a shameless matchmaker who didn't know when to quit.

"Weird, as usual," Arlen said with a small, restrained grin, though his mood was just as chipper as ever. "Can't talk much about it, sorry."

Darcy nodded, dropping his gaze to the bottle of glass cleaner he now clutched in a near death grip. "We know. It's all classified and stuff. Um—I've got to finish cleaning up. We had a major rush, and our counter looks pretty gross right now."

He spared the two a feeble smile of his own before turning back to the counter and spraying away, all too mindful of his overheated face as he worked. Arlen and Gloria continued to chat up Benjamin and Zoe when Darcy vanished in the back room to refill the now-empty spray bottle. He also took full advantage of that respite to regain his composure and settle himself with a few choice words of self-directed annoyance.

"What's the point? He's way out of your league. Why're you expecting him to settle?"

The jitters were soon gone following such a barrage of negativity, and Darcy was once again back in the comfortable and familiar headspace of not really liking himself so much. He nudged his glasses up his nose and stepped back outside, pleased to find the little shop finally empty of two powerful sorcerer-hunters. Zoe had also stepped out for a quick break, and Benjamin waited for him behind the counter, grinning ear-to-ear and dangling a small white paper bag—the shop's smallest bag used for individual chocolate pieces.

"This is yours," Benjamin said. "Mr. Cocky Hotshot bought you a couple of dark chocolate espresso truffles."

Darcy eyed the little bag dubiously, this time clutching the spray bottle of glass cleaner against his chest. "Me? Why?"

"Because he said you look like you needed some fattening up. Now take it before I kick you, goddamnit."

"No."

"Oh yeah? I guess you don't want to know what else Mr. Cocky Hotshot said about you while you were huddled in the back." When Darcy scowled at him, Benjamin snorted. "Okay, fine. He didn't say anything, but he kept staring at the door where you disappeared through. Totally intense, man. Like he was willing you to come back out, so he can carry you off like a crazy gay romantic hero and fuck you stupid."

Darcy sighed heavily, marched over to his boss, and snatched the bag of chocolate. "I'll eat this if it means you'll shut up about Arlen and romantic shit."

"Atta boy." Benjamin patted Darcy's hair like he would an eager little puppy who'd just piddled obediently in the grass. "Don't worry, I'm not into writing romance novels. I suck at that stuff. I'll keep my day job."

Chapter 2

"So did you get a reading?"

"Other than the obvious thing about that boy needing to eat something?"

Arlen snorted and gulped his iced tea as he and Gloria made their way down the busy commercial stretch. They'd just stopped by for coffee next door to Benjamin's chocolate shop, opting to save their chocolates for later. At least this time Arlen had gone for an actual box of chocolates that he could share with his friend.

"He's not a boy, obviously, you nut, and you know what I mean."

Gloria tittered. "I do, I do." She paused for a moment and responded in a more serious tone. "I did get a reading—who wouldn't have been able to? The residuals were so strong on him. You don't even have to try. I'm shocked he hasn't turned Ben's shop into a haunted chocolate factory whenever he clocks in for his shift."

"Yeah, that's what I thought. I wonder what the hell he's doing outside work to be practically drowning in residual energies like that," Arlen said after another pause. He frowned and took another big gulp of his iced tea, barely appreciating its soothing sweetness as they paused at an intersection and waited for the light to change.

"You've watched his house before," Gloria offered. "He never leaves, and you've only heard him play music late at night now and then. Do we still think he has some kind of weird magical talent that's somehow linked to his music? Remember those cases in Eastern Europe some hundreds of years ago?"

"The prodigies? I do, but—those cases involved public performances, didn't they? Darcy isn't even performing, and he's all alone when he plays."

"Maybe his music summons something?"

Arlen shook his head stubbornly. They were now headed back to where Gloria had parked her car, and from there they'd be on their way to the Arcane Institute for a quick briefing with their superiors.

"I sensed nothing, though, when I read his house—cabin. And I've already been there, what, five or six times in the last three weeks? I didn't see anything enter or exit at any time, didn't feel any weird fluctuations in my magic when I focused it on him. Nothing. It's bizarre."

Gloria held up her key fob and aimed, unlocking her car without breaking her stride. "I guess it'll have to be something for you to talk to Efrain about when we get back."

"You know, you could always use magic to unlock your car. I don't understand why you even bother with that stupid thing."

"Low tech's got its upsides, asshole."

"Low tech, my ass. Everything's computerized nowadays. Low tech's when you have to stick your key in the door and not need to have your car hooked up to a computer just so a mechanic can do a diagnostic on it."

Arlen spared Gloria a look and found his friend side-eyeing him with a smirk. "Oh, aren't you the old-fashioned type? Does Darcy know?"

Arlen rolled his eyes and turned his attention back to the sights and sounds of downtown Dolores. "Not interested, no time."

"Whatever."

Within moments they were inching their way through downtown traffic, with Arlen's thoughts still fixed on the young man he'd left behind in the chocolate shop. Darcy Winter was a cipher—had always been one to Arlen. There was something about Darcy, who looked more like a scrawny teenager than a twenty-one-year-old, that plucked insistently at the periphery of Arlen's mind.

Otherworldly essences always, *always* surrounded Darcy whenever they crossed paths. Those essences or residuals were also so shockingly strong that Arlen pictured Darcy as somehow being submerged in the world of the dead in the past—recent or otherwise—and those unnatural imprints had soaked into his bones and had become a normal part of him.

That Darcy appeared not to realize the peculiarity of his condition and continued to go about his day-to-day business with the same amount of quiet resignation only stoked Arlen's urge to be more watchful around him. Darcy, at least to Arlen, made for a pretty fascinating case study, though Arlen wouldn't even know where to begin when it came to analyzing the mystery Darcy dangled before him.

And it was because the most baffling and exasperating part about all of that was the fact that those residuals were extremely elusive when it came to identifying them. They weren't of the mortal world, yes, but besides that fact—nothing. And no amount of watching and reading done on the tiny, old-fashioned cabin where Darcy lived alone helped.

Arlen could always look away and turn his attention to something more worth his time in pursuing, but something continued to niggle at the back of his mind with a subtle urgency, putting a stop to the temptation to move on. And it had nothing to do with the sadness in Darcy's eyes whenever he looked at Arlen.

* * * *

The Institute of Arcane Studies was considered an Ivy League school dedicated to the intensive study and practice of light magic in all its forms. The institute boasted one of the most impressive rosters of highly trained sorcerer-hunters in the American continent, half of whom were prodigies in their fields of expertise. Having been tested young after showing natural talents that often couldn't be measured, these chosen few graduated much younger than their predecessors.

They, in turn, gave rise to theories regarding newer generations of sorcerer-hunters being a great deal more powerful than before. Though as to why, no one had yet to determine.

An equal amount of relief came with the confusion, however, as the newest generation of magic-wielders were much more attuned to technology and were able to keep its dangerous effects on the world of mortals and the otherworld at a minimum. Some elders had half-jokingly claimed that the saints and the gods who kept a selfish watch over their mortal representatives had also learned how technology worked. They'd then adapted accordingly, blessing their champions with skills and a supernatural reach that were beyond comprehension.

And a few generations from then? Who knew what abilities sorcerers would have? For the time being, sorcerer-hunters and their peers simply went about their work and suffered through the unpalatability of cafeteria dreck—like other university students and faculty, one supposed.

"That's not hexed. It's pretty safe to eat."

Arlen sighed and glanced up to regard Efrain Thorley, another sorcerer-hunter who'd been hired as an auxiliary master (or adjunct faculty). Efrain, at least, had the benefit of a sweet, live-in boyfriend who doted on him and spoiled him rotten with home-cooked meals, which Efrain would pack for work. Arlen couldn't say the same for himself.

"It's pretty scary-looking spaghetti," Arlen replied glumly, demonstrating his unhappiness by poking the soggy pasta with his plastic fork. "I'll bet you the meat's still alive. If you listen closely, you'll probably hear it talking to you. Not even sure if this really *is* meat, to be honest."

Efrain blinked. "Leander's right. You need a boyfriend."

"Don't even start." Arlen scowled and snorted, certain a puff of smoke just blew out of his nostrils—like a cartoon bull. "It'll take a hell of a lot of hexing to get someone to put up with me."

Arlen knew too well his reputation as a goody-two-shoes stick-in-the-mud type who tended to get a wee bit obsessive about his work to the detriment of simple, day-to-day things like hygiene or even nutrition. As a trainee in the Advanced Arcane Program throughout his teenage years, he'd all but wasted away. He'd given his studies too much of his attention and focus that faculty mentors, thoroughly alarmed, had descended upon him with healing and restful spells on their lips.

In the end, Arlen found himself grounded by a very irate set of parents who nearly pulled their son from the Arcane Institute for his sake. And he did end up getting sick from neglect (or self-neglect, at any rate).

Now, at twenty-three, he could swear his ears still rang from his mother's furious shrieking and scolding from back in the day. He'd improved somewhat, though his life skills were largely limited to laundry and brewing coffee, hence his continued living in his parents' home and his parents' incessant grumbling for a "nice boy who can turn ours into something remotely human". He still couldn't make a decent sandwich if his life depended on it, let alone cook himself a real, honest-to-goodness dish—like spaghetti.

"Well, we need to find someone who'd be willing to be hexed on your account first."

"Ha-fucking-ha. Anyway, we're supposed to be talking about stuff."

"Darcy Winter, you mean."

Arlen's scowl deepened. "I don't like the way your eyes shine whenever you say his name. It's creepy."

Efrain didn't look a bit sorry and in fact appeared smug as he casually cut a small piece of the grilled salmon Leander had made for that day's lunch. "Anyway, Darcy Winter—lots of residuals, still no definite reading of what they are, eh?"

"That's the long and short of it, yeah. I don't get it. I swear I've staked out his cabin for almost a month now, on and off at random days, and still nothing. I'm this close to breaking in and going full stalker mode just to find out if something dangerous is up."

"Dude, you're already on full stalker mode now." Efrain snorted and pursed his lips as he considered things. "You know what his history is, though?"

"No. He lives in that ancient cabin, which I know he'd inherited from his mom, and that's about it. Hell, I never expected anyone to live in something like that here in Dolores. I mean, seriously, a cabin? Like a vacation cabin in the mountain? Then again, his home's like way out there—like outside the city but still in the city limits."

"What got your attention, anyway? You kind of spotted him while shopping for groceries or something?"

Arlen blinked. "How'd you know that?"

"Wild guess. Jesus, dude, everyone's got to eat. Even Darcy has to come out of hiding and get something for his food. Besides, residuals aside, he's still a normal guy—works a pretty decent job, giving your stalker ass an excuse to stop by the chocolate shop and get something you likely don't even need." Efrain paused and looked around them. "Speaking of, what did you do with the chocolates you got? Don't tell me you ate them all."

"No, Gloria did. I kind of owed her." Arlen sighed again, heavily this time, and sat back. "So how do I move forward with this? I can always leave him alone, but you know I can't. There could be something up with him, and for all we know, he might have opened a door to the otherworld without knowing it." And Arlen couldn't see quiet, withdrawn Darcy Winter somehow engaging dark forces from the other side on purpose. He couldn't—and he simply wouldn't.

"Look into his history, then. You've only been aware of him for, what, a month now?"

Arlen knew his friend was right. He knew absolutely nothing about Darcy Winter other than superficial readings of residuals as well as brief observations of the young man at work. If he wished to get a better sense of a real threat, he needed to up his game.

"Guess I'll have to do some research on his family history," he muttered, grimacing as he continued to poke at his food.

"Or you can always talk to him? Just a thought. He might have a germ of something to offer you, and you can work with it. And I'm sure you'll just be a total badass about it."

"Nope. Not going there. I don't want to give him ideas about me and what I'm really doing when I try to talk to him."

Efrain sighed. "Do you think he's exposed to some kind of danger without realizing it?"

"I think so. I mean—I wouldn't be surprised if he were."

"Okay, well—ball's in your court."

Arlen shrugged and braved a forkful of spaghetti. His friend was right, of course. Arlen needed to start somewhere, and he tried not to think too much of his options at that moment, especially when he had a mouthful of surprisingly decent-tasting cafeteria food.

Chapter 3

St. Anthony's looked awfully wretched that day, Darcy thought as he peered out of his kitchen windows. The day was bright and sunny, though the shifting of the colors of the leaves marked the changing seasons. Autumn was around the corner, and soon the days would be far too short. And Darcy wouldn't be able to visit St. Anthony's when the need arose.

He frowned, drumming his fingers on the kitchen counter, before deciding to go out and take care of his neighbors.

Darcy's cabin—yes, a tiny, one-bedroom cabin with a sizable attic space that had been turned into a garret room (and Darcy's bedroom back in the day when his mother still lived)—stood well beyond the last line of houses marking the residential periphery of Dolores. It was still within city limits, in fact only several yards away from those invisible boundaries, but one might as well wonder if they'd just stepped into a wholly different place altogether once they drove through the more wooded and rural fringes of a bustling city.

The cabin stood alone as well, and it was located within walking distance of an ancient and tiny cemetery long abandoned and forgotten. Ironically named after the patron saint of lost objects, St. Anthony's had always been a part of Darcy's legacy, turning him into a caretaker of sorts. He'd always felt obligated to look after it, anyway, the mothers' visits an ongoing reminder of abandonment in death. And because of their weekly lullabies, Darcy constantly wondered if he was the only person who mourned those poor, nameless souls and offered them comfort through his music.

Darcy finished wiping down the counter and set the rag aside for laundry. The cabin's small side door was between the water heater and the kitchen counter, and he snatched the large plastic bucket off the floor, his thick gardening gloves tucked inside along with his trusty pair of overworked hedge shears, and a box of lawn bags.

The rusty iron gates of St. Anthony's had long fallen into disrepair, and they stood unlocked and partly open, the gap wide enough for Darcy to move through with some effort but without too much trouble. The gate itself was crooked and slightly bent in places, which only exacerbated its inability to be properly shut against the world.

Inside the wrought iron fence encircling the cemetery, invasive vines and weeds embraced cracked and broken gravestones. The ground was barely even felt underfoot, with more overgrown grass and the like packing the spaces in between graves. A couple of cemetery angels rose above the mass of vines, their serene countenances marred by moss-blackened and broken stone.

Somewhere in the middle of the cemetery, Darcy knew, stood an old vault where a nameless family had once thought to bury their dead. It was now nothing more than a sad above-ground tomb whose brick-covered entry had pretty much been further secured from violators by the growth of thick vines all over it.

He'd yet to find out who was interred there, what moneyed family had been able to afford what must have been a pricey tomb. There were no names anywhere identifying the vault's residents. Not even a plaque or a nearly obliterated carving of letters he could have deciphered existed anywhere on the vault's crumbling walls. It sometimes made him wonder if the sarcophagus within was empty or if there even was one, let alone more.

All the same, the mysterious burial vault and its forlorn neighbors all suffered from the same levels of abandonment and neglect. Wealth meant absolutely nothing where death was concerned.

Darcy walked a little distance before planting himself in tangled, knee-high vines and grass. He blinked as he looked around him, taking in the familiar sights of gravestones, overgrowth, and slender, balding trees. Something felt off about the place, and while he knew others who wouldn't have the same connection he had with St. Anthony's would simply consider an old cemetery choking on vegetation to be off in so many ways, he knew there was something that didn't belong somehow.

Was that it? A certain alien element had somehow worked itself into a sad relic of the past?

He bent all thought on this curious sensation, holding his breath as he fought to read it. Was it something alive? Life in death? Whatever it might be, it was proving to be rather elusive despite Darcy's efforts.

He couldn't see anything different, even when he trudged forward, taking a random path through the thick vegetation and uneven ground. He paused here and there, craning his neck and moving his gaze back and forth many times over, even straining his ears and sniffing the air for anything that could indicate something that didn't belong.

He could see, hear, or smell nothing unusual. The same crushing loneliness met his gaze in those weathered gravestones. The same silence and occasional birdsong or slight breeze softly grazed his hearing. The same scents of grass, wood, and old stone could be smelled.

And yet he sensed something askew about St. Anthony's.

The sudden rumble of a car tearing down the road some distance hence broke his near trance, and with a sigh and a puzzled shrug, Darcy started his "maintenance" of the cemetery. He set his bucket down, pulled on his thick gloves, and proceeded to trim some excessive vines and weeds. It was, in many ways, a monumental task for a single person to take on despite the relative smallness of St. Anthony's, for the cemetery was home to no more than a dozen graves. But the neglect and the toll of the years on the poor little patch of land were awfully heavy, and Darcy had long learned not to cover the entire cemetery if he could help it. Some cleaning up until he was too tired to do more was all he could manage, and he took some measure of comfort in it. At least someone took the trouble of looking after the forgotten dead.

He allowed himself an hour that day, filling his bucket perhaps five or six times and emptying it into a lawn bag before deciding to throw in the towel.

"I hope this is enough for now," he said, wiping his forehead with his sleeve and looking around him one last time. "I have to work tomorrow, and my schedule's going to be kind of off for a week. I might not be back for a while. Hope you all don't mind."

He finished his work quite a distance from the main entrance, and when he picked up the full bucket and turned to stumble back toward home, a sound caught his attention, and he paused. He glanced behind him and saw nothing, of course. Another thorough scan of the immediate area revealed nothing, either.

"Huh."

Probably the wind, he thought, but the air barely moved the whole time he worked, and it remained still even then. He turned and walked a few more paces before the sound broke the silence again.

"Hello? Anyone here?" he called, scowling now.

As before, nothing answered him, and the cemetery was once more silent.

Darcy suddenly felt the hair up and down his body stand on end as he contemplated the sounds. They were both the same, and they made him turn his attention in the direction of the cemetery's center, where the single burial vault stood. From where he was, he could glimpse its mossy and vine-infested walls and roof past the collection of slender trees.

"Hello? Uh—this is a private cemetery, and you can get into trouble trespassing!"

Darcy thought nothing about lying, but he needed a response. Again, he received nothing.

For a moment he dithered where he stood, wondering if he ought to brave it and go to the vault and see for himself if someone, indeed, had broken into that old thing. It was obviously impossible, of course, but the sound he thought he heard somehow insisted it wasn't.

At length he decided to give it a go, taking comfort in the late morning sunshine and warmth.

He trudged forward, weaving his way past leaning and overgrown gravestones till he found himself standing directly before the old vault's stairs. The crumbling stone steps numbered about nine, he knew, having gone down before but finding himself locked out by the vine-covered entryway. He inched closer to the top of the steps and looked down, not at all surprised to see nothing wrong. In addition to pieces of broken stone littering the steps and the bottom floor, there were small branches and stray leaves and weeds dirtying up the vault's entrance.

He shuddered at the sight. The vault was made entirely of brick and mortar, unevenly put together and covered originally in more concrete that had long crumbled off and exposed significant areas of the underlying brickwork. The vault had always made him think of horror stories involving people getting bricked up alive.

"Anyone down there?" he called again, and he gingerly walked down the steps.

It was ridiculous calling out that question, and he knew it. At this point, Darcy simply functioned on automatic, unease goading him on and stunting all efforts at rational thought. Something deeper, something he couldn't quite shake off, however, convinced him he was on the right track, the tiny, whispering voice in the back of his mind nearly incoherent in its nervous stuttering.

Then again, the mere presence of the old vault always made his imagination run wildly in the worst possible ways.

Perhaps the sounds he heard had been nothing more than a natural phenomenon, though he'd yet to fully comprehend what it was or what it sounded like. It had been too distant and too muffled for any easy grab at clarity or understanding. It could also be the stifling silence that had played tricks on his senses.

He toyed with the possibility of a chink developing in the vault's masonry somehow, and a bit of air had blown through it, creating that strange sound. A sigh? A groan? Darcy couldn't tell, and as he tried to come up with something good and solid to which he could compare the sound, he found he still fell short. It had been too brief to be fully taken in by his senses and given a bit of processing in his mind.

Darcy headed back up and was soon standing outside St. Anthony's, emptying the contents of his bucket into the lawn bag for the last time that day. He glanced in the direction of the road as a few more cars and a truck rumbled past, and he didn't realize till then just how welcome those sounds were.

His original plan for the day was to spend a lengthier amount of time tending the cemetery, but that strange moment convinced him to take it easy instead. If what he'd just experienced was nothing more than the product of a tired and overworked brain, he was quite justified in giving himself a bit of a break.

After setting the lawn bag against the side of the cabin for the following morning's pick up, Darcy locked himself away in his home and showered.

He was putting together a chicken sandwich when he suddenly felt the unnerving urge to check all of the windows and doors of his little cabin and ensuring they were fully locked and secured against the outside world. He didn't know why he had to do it, but an insistent voice in the back of his mind wouldn't let up. He even felt obligated to hurry up to the loft and ensure the two little windows there were also secured.

And when he finished putting his lunch together, he looked up and out of his kitchen window.

St. Anthony's looked the same as ever—innocuous despite its wretched state. Yet a faint unease rippled through Darcy as he regarded the cemetery in the distance, and he had to pull the short curtains of the windows close, blocking the sight. He didn't care if it darkened his kitchen and dining area a little. As long as he didn't have to see the cemetery while standing at the counter, he could manage a bit of muted light in the midday.

From there he searched for his phone, turned on his favorite music app, and brought up the volume.

"There," he murmured as he set the phone on one of the bookshelves. "Much better."

The lively sounds of music fusing Delta blues, jazz, and 1930s swing filled the cabin and easily tore the curtain of his earlier unease off Darcy's mind. In another moment he was singing along while sweeping the floor, pausing now and then to throw in an awkward dance move and laughing at himself while he was at it.

Chapter 4

Arlen eyed the map dubiously, pursing his lips as he considered. What an odd place to put a cemetery, he thought, and a tiny one at that. Using "standard urban guidelines"—as he'd always called them—he reckoned the distance between Darcy's cabin and the cemetery was about two-and-a-half or closer to three blocks.

The space between was also pretty devoid of intervening vegetation that could have blocked Darcy's view of St. Anthony's. There were only patchy grass and weeds marred by a rough foot path, quite likely formed from years of back and forth movement between cabin and cemetery.

St. Anthony's itself continued to elude him.

The public library had absolutely nothing on the place, with every map Arlen could find not once indicating that specific area for anything other than an untouched section of Dolores's rural fringes. The only cemetery worth historians' attention was the city's main one, and it was located farther away. On the opposite end of the city, in fact.

Equally surprising was the fact that librarians appeared to be only peripherally aware of the cemetery's existence as well. And it was only because they'd driven down that one isolated road that went past Darcy's cabin and St. Anthony's a few times. That road took cars out of the city proper and into the vast, tree-peppered meadows and low, rolling hills before hitting the nearest northbound freeway, which skirted the glorious California coast. It was a longer and more winding route to the freeway, but it was also the more picturesque one.

According to the librarians, they only knew of the cemetery upon glancing out the window of their cars. For a handful of seconds, they could see the barely visible iron fence and whatever dilapidated stone monument happened to rise above the tops of the jungle of vines and trees. It was, in truth, too hard to see and, therefore, too easy to forget. And that was simply that.

Darcy's cabin, however, had been duly noted and judged "adorable" and "quaint". There had even been whispers of turning it into a structure of historical interest, but some knots over legalities kept anyone from pursuing it. From what little Arlen could gather, it had everything to do with Darcy's ownership and some sort of legally binding contract made a couple of centuries ago between the city and the cabin's original owner.

Most likely Darcy's ancestor, Arlen decided, but he was getting ahead of himself by mulling over this point and forced his attention back to the librarians' rambling accounts from earlier. Which was, sadly, about the cemetery's existence or non-existence in the main library's archives and whether or not magic had any say in its strange situation.

And if anyone did agree to its existence, they'd always claimed it stood directly on the city's border, which may or may not mean anything significant in the world of magic. It was a new border, really, the area designated to Dolores being much larger in the distant past. There'd been disputes, arguments going back and forth over the true city limits in those parts, and eventually, the newer city limits were agreed upon and drawn, a great deal closer than before.

Arlen had always considered those details awfully tedious to keep track of, but he valued the librarians' eager sharing of obscure facts. Whether or not they'd offer him something concrete to work with, he'd yet to find out.

He sat back with a tired sigh, crossing his arms over his chest as he glowered magnificently at the map—as though by doing so, he could somehow wrest some of St. Anthony's secrets out.

Funny, he thought, how such a thing like location and its possible significance had never even crossed his mind. He'd only observed St. Anthony's from a very objective distance, and his impression was that of complete and hopeless isolation. He suspected it to be a tiny cemetery, too, which might mean someone had started it with concrete plans for its future and had abandoned it for some reason.

"How goes the info hunting?"

Arlen looked up to eye a ruefully smiling Gloria. She held a couple of large cups of iced mocha—Arlen's favorite cold drug—topped with whipped cream and a generous sprinkling of cocoa powder.

"Does this mean I owe you another box of chocolate? That's kind of unfair, considering how much I pay for that stuff."

Gloria only rolled her eyes and thrust Arlen's drink under his nose. "Shut up and take it. And answer my question."

She was always so bossy, but she was also like his big sister in a way. Older than Arlen by a good five years, she was a veteran in the sorcerer-hunter business before Arlen was accepted into the program. And she always fussed over him in that grumpy, bossy, older sister sort of way that made other people grin and go "Aww".

"It's just weird," he said after taking a couple of massive gulps of his drink. He tapped the map with his pen. "St. Anthony's might as well not exist at all."

"Is that why no one ever knew about it all this time? That's kind of impossible, considering how old that cemetery looks. What do you think—maybe two hundred years? Three hundred, even?"

"Closer to three hundred, maybe. Never been there, but I imagine the gravestones can't that bad. Broken and messed up over time, sure, but still standing. So somewhere between two and three hundred years?"

Gloria nodded and made a quiet, thoughtful sound. "You think there's a link between that and the cabin somehow? The footpath shows movement between the two places, and it's really a worn-down trail from people walking over the grass so many times."

Arlen leaned back in his chair and cudgeled his brain. "I'm guessing the cabin's old, but not as old as the cemetery. It's pretty likely something else used to stand there, and it just got torn down after X number of years. So—I don't know—caretakers? You know, people who looked after the cemetery used to live in that previous house? That can explain the footpath."

He had to append, however, that the cabin could have easily undergone upgrades and renovations over the years, considering how clearly it withstood Nature's perpetually shifting moods. He'd seen wreckages of structures hailing from the days of the Old West, and Darcy's cabin practically had the glamour and shine of a mansion in comparison.

He wouldn't be surprised if older forms of magic played a key role in the cabin's preservation.

"And it can explain why the cemetery's pretty much fallen apart over time if those caretakers died or moved away." Gloria glanced at him, brows raised. "Have you ever seen Darcy go to St. Anthony's?"

"No. But then again, I've only scoped out his cabin at night."

Ghosts, revenants, what have you—anything finding its way through the veil separating the otherworld from the world of mortals were always active at night, though there were always exceptions to the rule. They found strength in darkness, and they also took advantage of the cover of night to creep about, haunting people's steps or homes. While most of the ghosts sorcerer-hunters dispatched were nothing more than melancholy echoes of their live selves, others displayed some degree of conscious thought, and those were the ones the Institute of Arcane Studies was concerned about the most.

And now it seemed Arlen had unwittingly stumbled across another kind of haunting. Or at least another kind of influence from the otherworld. And that involved what he now referred to as a "dormant essence", which made him think of a dormant gene. It seemed as though Darcy Winter, in supernatural terms, carried some kind of dormant influence from the otherworld, one that could still somehow find expression through some triggering situation. As to what could happen? So many different possibilities existed, most of them dangerous and terrifying.

That Darcy himself appeared not to be aware of anything only added to the element of danger as far as Arlen was concerned.

"Maybe you should look into his family history. I wonder if he's a descendant of St. Anthony's caretakers if those people existed before. I wouldn't be surprised if he turned out to be one," Gloria piped up after a moment's ponderous silence.

Arlen made a face. "Stalker status just got upgraded," he grumbled. "But I know what you mean."

"Talk to him. Ask him out on a date or something."

"You're nuts. I'm not going to lead him on. That's fucked up."

Arlen might be an absolute obsessive when it came to his work, but he wasn't *that* into his work. Poor Darcy, he thought, though his mood simultaneously surged at the idea of getting closer than what he'd been used to with Darcy.

"I know. I was just messing with you." Gloria considered. "Then just chat him up. Try to get to know him better. If you don't want to lead him on, all you need to do is make sure you keep him at arm's length. Should be easy for you. I've seen you do it a gajillion times before. It's like second nature to you."

"Are you saying I'm a cold bastard?"

"Pretty much, yeah."

Gloria appended that with a loud slurp of her drink while fluttering her eyelashes at Arlen, who could only glare at her. A quick sip of his iced mocha easily took care of the sting, but he knew she was telling the truth, anyway.

"Let's check out the cemetery," he said at length. "Darcy should be at work right now, and that means there's no one hanging around St. Anthony's or keeping an eye on it."

Gloria blinked. "So you think he's been watching the cemetery—like, you know, a caretaker would. Even though you said you've never seen him go there before."

"Seeing him go there is different from thinking that he's been there," Arlen replied with a heavy, tired sigh. "Are we splitting straws or something? It sure feels like it."

Gloria laughed and reached across the small table to pat Arlen's hand. "Just finish your damn drink, lover boy. We'll figure something out. Oh, by the way, we'll have to choose another day to check out the cemetery together. I've got a ton of laundry to do."

"You slacked off for a week again, didn't you?"

"Yeah, well. Shit happens."

Once she left, Arlen was again alone with his thoughts, which were no less jumbled than before. Around him the rest of the trainees and lecturers moved in an easy swarm, the Arcane Institute's cafeteria proving more and more to be the worst place for him to mull things over. He should be in the institute's library, going over its archives, chasing every possibility that popped up.

The map over which he'd been tearing his hair out was one he'd checked out of the public library. Not that the Arcane Institute's own collection boasted something different as he'd been over their maps before hitting the public library for theirs. Not even magic-wielders from decades past knew anything about the cemetery, apparently.

But that, however, didn't discount other sources. Perhaps hidden somewhere in the Arcane Institute's dusty archives was a book—hopefully two or even more—going over some of the more obscure historical events in Dolores.

One or two books in a collection numbering a thousand at the very least, half of which were originally from Europe, Africa, and Asia, he immediately appended, dismay piling upon dismay. Where would he even start? A plea-prayer to the library's guardian ought to help because he'd rather not get anything started with Darcy.

If anybody—or anything—could help him, it would be the institute's strange archivist. With any luck, Arlen would go to its counter with cap in hand, and that would be enough to convince the prickly ageless spirit to help out one of the institute's own.

Chapter 5

"Oh, hey—didn't know you shop here."

Darcy gave a little start and spun around, nearly crushing his bag of groceries against his chest. It took him half a moment to gather himself, blinking owlishly at a grinning Arlen Stroescu, who held the ubiquitous cup of iced coffee piled high with all the fixings. Arlen also carried his messenger bag crossbody, all in all adding to his look of young G-man of some sort. At least he didn't wear a pair of shades this time.

"Uh—hi," Darcy stammered, quickly and awkwardly adjusting his glasses, which had slipped down his nose from the sudden jolt. "I just finished. Um—yeah, I usually buy my groceries here. I'm on my way home."

Arlen nodded and indicated the bag, which seemed to grow heavier by the second. "I can carry that for you," he said. "We can switch. If you don't mind holding on to my liquid drug."

"I can carry this just fine. I've done it before, you know, and I've got a folding trolley I use all the time." Darcy quickly backtracked, coloring, once he realized what a jerk move he'd just made. "Sorry. I didn't mean to snap at you. I really can haul my groceries on my own. I don't live far."

Things seemed to take a wee while to sink in, with Arlen frowning at first before widening his eyes in horror. "You walk home with all that? I thought you live a couple more miles out!"

"Wait, what? How'd you know that?"

"Ah. I—someone told me. Because, you know, I kind of asked."

"Why?"

Arlen appeared to fumble a bit, his handsome features turning all shades of red, orange, and even purple. He took a couple of huge slurps of his drink before his mind seemed to right itself, and he was once again on form.

"Because I was curious. I know Ben and Zoe, but I don't really know you as well. And seeing as how I'm like a regular customer of Ben's chocolate shop, it's kind of nice if I get to know everyone there. You know, I've got a car. I can drive you home. I don't mind, really. I mean, what kind of person am I that I'd let you walk home with that load and not offer you any help? Right?"

Darcy could only gape at him, utterly mystified by the bizarre workings of Arlen's mind. He could practically hear the wild spinning of cogs and gears in that phenomenal skull of his, given the way Arlen's flow of thoughts seemed to follow a pretty insane, labyrinthine path without slowing down.

The grocery store he'd gone to was a small, family-run outfit located nearest to Darcy's cabin. His mother had always gone there, and with his transportation situation not at all improving, Darcy took it as a no-brainer. A number of shoppers crammed the small store, forcing Darcy to step outside and onto the old-fashioned wooden sidewalk. There he'd left his foldable shopping trolley, which he'd secured against one of the wooden benches lining the sidewalk.

As he set his bag down on the bench and knelt to undo the lock, Darcy's face burned from the mortification of realizing just how ridiculous it was, locking up a cheap, aluminum shopping cart. He had no choice, after all, that being his one and only means of conveying a two-week supply of food and non-edibles, no matter what the weather. He never learned how to ride a bicycle or drive a car, so he depended entirely on the bus or his feet to take him from one place to another. And that disadvantage had never once bothered him—until now, anyway.

Pride also refused to be overruled, and a touch of anger made his movements clumsy and inarticulate. After an eternity, he finally had his groceries secured in the trolley, and he made a move down one direction of the sidewalk, toward the wheelchair access ramp. He said nary a word to Arlen and wished the man would just give up and go.

"You mean to say you walk, what, two or three miles with a cart of groceries all the time?" Arlen blurted out, incredulous, and Darcy had to sigh.

"Yeah. I don't have a choice. The bus doesn't even go that far, so it's kind of pointless for me to take it with this much stuff with me. And it's only two miles. Seriously, I'm used to it."

"What do you do when it rains?"

"I have a tarp cover thing that I use to protect my groceries." And before Arlen could ask another question, he quickly added, "And I wear a really hardcore raincoat. It's all good. I'm used to it, and nobody should have to worry about me over—you know—how I do my usual errands and stuff."

Of course, he wouldn't dare say anything about how storms tended to affect Darcy's plans of adequate sustenance. Over the years, he'd learned the hard way to stock up on canned food, frozen macaroni and cheese dinners, snack bars, and toilet paper in anticipation of being grounded by torrential rain for a number of days.

Darcy kept his mind fixed on his destination, though he remained acutely aware of Arlen's presence, which had caught up with him and now stayed abreast. Distressingly, the breeze picked up and tantalized Darcy's olfactory senses with a subtle whiff of Arlen's cologne. The man wore cologne? Darcy had to sigh inwardly. Of course, he would. Arlen Stroescu dressed like a male model to work, so it stood to reason he'd work a bit of masculine fragrance in there to complete the fashion magazine look. Not that Darcy was complaining, but the cologne sure didn't help the near wreckage of his thoughts.

And to find oneself suddenly the center of attention of someone as devastatingly handsome as Arlen? It only made his irritation and confusion worse.

"Don't you have to go back to the Arcane Institute?" Darcy asked, sparing his bewildered and bewildering companion a halfway exasperated glance. "You don't have to stay with me."

"Well—do you shop at night or something? I hope not, especially if you walk home with your groceries like this."

Was there a sincere edge of worry in Arlen's voice? Darcy might have misheard him considering how much his own mind struggled to find some solid footing. The conversation was throwing him off his center in spectacular manner, and he plain didn't know just how best to deal with it.

"No. I usually work till six and then go straight home. And—what do you take me for, anyway? I'm not stupid."

"I never said you were."

They'd walked about half a block by now, with foot traffic nearly gone as they'd reached the fringes of Dolores's downtown area. It was the one part of the city that ended abruptly, in a way, with no houses or apartments somehow marking the outer perimeter thereabouts. The stores merely appeared older and older with every block away from the city's busier center.

That part of Dolores, anyway, mirrored the Old West with some of its buildings, and rumor had it the final three blocks boasted the original structures from those days, remnants of a small town and far simpler times. In his increasingly muddled state, Darcy had to turn his focus to them as a temporary distraction in order to clear his head.

He'd checked out just about every store housed in what might have been an old saloon or even brothel in the distant past, but even he knew a con when he saw it. Faked weathering, vintage fixtures—the works. The buildings might look Old West, but he could see everything was all for show. In the end, he decided that part of the city merely reflected the diversity of a city long mired in old legends, magic, and modern technology, even if what it showcased was nothing more than faux Gold Rush chic.

He stumbled to a halt and turned to glare at Arlen.

"What do you need, Arlen?" he demanded. "You never used to bother me like this before."

Arlen, bless his heart, looked absolutely baffled. He blinked, slurped, looked around, and then fixed his attention back on Darcy with the same air of confusion.

"Bother you? Am I bothering you?" he stammered.

Darcy nearly cried "yes", but he checked himself. No, Arlen wasn't actually bothering him. If he were honest with himself, he'd admit how much he liked it when Arlen paid attention to him like this, considering how much of a crush Darcy had always had on the man. That said, Arlen seemed to be uncomfortable hanging around Darcy, which also threw a gigantic bucket of icy water on his hopes.

Arlen was never a sociable sort, from what Darcy had observed and from what he'd been told. He felt uncomfortable being around people and forced into small talk. Arlen was merely one of those who thrived in solitary work, channeling every ounce of focus and energy into whatever task was at hand. Arlen got things done with the expertise and efficiency of someone far older and more experienced, and he simply had no time for frivolous pursuits outside the tiny, tiny circle of friends who could bear with him.

At length, when he realized he'd hesitated too long, Darcy sighed heavily and shrugged, dropping his gaze to his faded and ragged old sneakers, which looked about fifty years older than Arlen's polished leather oxfords. Good lord, the man dressed like a high end office stiff, Darcy thought, mortification growing at the yawning social chasm between them.

"No, you're not. Sorry. It's just that—I guess I'm not used to getting this much attention from anyone, especially you." He shrugged again, helplessly this time. "I don't mean to be rude."

"Well—uh—I really do want to help you with your groceries. Um—will you go out with me?"

"Huh? What? Did you—like a date?"

When Darcy glanced up, wide-eyed and stunned, he saw Arlen smile ruefully and blush, though he didn't shuffle from foot to foot in a show of embarrassment. Self-consciousness rolled off him in heavy waves, but he still appeared as held together as ever. Darcy had to admit to being absolutely impressed by Arlen's show of control.

"Yeah, I guess. Like a date," Arlen replied, the smile easing into a broader and brighter one that indicated a return of his usual confidence. He drank his coffee, waiting with utmost patience for Darcy to say something back.

"But why?"

"Because?" Arlen laughed softly now, eyes twinkling merrily as he continued to pin an increasingly flustered Darcy with a keen gaze. "Seriously, because I want to have dinner with you. Or lunch, whichever you prefer. Hell, even breakfast in the afternoon would be perfect if that's what you like."

Darcy could only stare at him in drop-jawed confusion and helplessness.

Arlen, still chuckling, reached out his free hand and gently nudged Darcy's chin up, forcing his mouth to close. "So—what you do say? Will you go out with me?"

"Um—I guess? Oh, I mean, yes? Sorry, that didn't come out right the first time around."

Arlen's smile brightened even more, if such a thing were even possible at this point. "Okay. How about if I pick you up from work tomorrow night?"

"Okay, that's fine. Tomorrow night. Yeah."

"I'll see you tomorrow, Darcy. Enjoy your walk home." Arlen winked at him then before walking off and leaving Darcy staring at him in stupefied silence.

"What the hell just happened?" Darcy muttered, blinking.

Arlen wove his way through the thin crowd, every stride sure, his bearings oozing with a simmering power that left Darcy damned near salivating where he stood. It took him a moment to collect his thoughts again, and he eventually remembered, rather painfully, he still had a bit of a distance to cover on foot.

Once he reached his cabin, everything seemed to fly in a muddy haze, leaving him standing in the middle of the dining area blinking in mute surprise and looking around him quizzically. He couldn't even remember what he'd just done other than put his groceries away, and even then, what he could recall of his actual movements felt so distant and dream-like.

Damn Arlen and his insidious effects on Darcy.

"Okay, fine."

Casting a black look in the general direction of the store where Arlen managed to wring a "yes" from him, Darcy huffed, spun on his heel, and marched upstairs. He took up his cello, dragged his chair to the middle of the garret room, plunked his backside on it, and proceeded to play.

He'd plucked Waldteufel's "The Skater's Waltz" randomly in his head. He must have made a right hash of the piece, and he wouldn't be surprised if he did. And it was because Arlen kept interfering with his concentration by appearing in Darcy's head as a Victorian gentleman ice skating happily somewhere. And still looking as ridiculously handsome as ever.

Darcy shook his head at himself, scowling at his bow. "Christ, I'm hopeless," he muttered.

Chapter 6

"Wow. That was smooth."

Arlen glowered at Gloria, who regarded him with a vaguely disappointed and resigned look. "Have you been spying on me?"

"Well, yeah—I sent Benitez out to keep an eye on you. Seriously, Arlen, I thought you were going to just chat him up. I remember you going weird on me over the possibility of dating the poor guy." Gloria paused, now appearing disappointed and doubtful. "You did what, though? Benitez was a little—frazzled—when he reported back. I think you completely threw him off his game, and he came back to me in shock. Now I'm confused."

Benitez. Of course. Arlen rolled his eyes at the obvious point. He should have known Gloria would be sending her familiar, a crow named Benitez, out to watch over him when he told her he was setting off to look for Darcy. Benitez was a nosy little monster of a bird, at that, which meant every stammer, every blush, every twitch, and every nervous slurp of his iced coffee drink would be taken in and reported to his sorcerer-hunter.

"I kind of have a date with him now, yes."

"Back up, back up. You really asked him out on a date? I thought you don't do dates."

Arlen sighed, scrubbing his eyes tiredly with his fingers. "I wasn't going to, but I panicked. He was starting to get defensive and all that, and I didn't know how to keep him from running away, so I asked him out."

In truth, Darcy was apologizing for being rude when Arlen blurted out his request for a date. And while Arlen really was afraid of having Darcy walk away from him, he posed his awkward question because he hated seeing the young man so miserable. It had only been a day since, yet Arlen continued to feel the hurt.

He'd asked Darcy out on a date because he felt sorry for him. It would have to be one of—if not *the*—stupidest move he'd ever done in his life. It was wrong on so many levels that Arlen didn't even know where to start.

Gloria's look of disappointment and resignation turned into a narrow-eyed, dubious stare. "Arlen, your social skills suck ass," she said, acid dripping from every vowel, every consonant. "You don't ask someone for a date when that someone starts to get edgy around you. You back off."

Arlen threw his hands up. "God, you're acting as though I've never gone out on a date before. I've been out with at least a couple of guys before—like back in my late teens. And if you *must* know, I also had sex with them. I thought my dick was going to shrivel up and drop off before I got my diploma."

"I really didn't *have* to know, but it's too late for that now." Gloria sighed and gave Arlen a light slap on the shoulder. "Just be careful, okay? I'm more worried about him than you. Don't break his heart."

Arlen grimaced. It was a little too late for that now, too, he thought, shoving his hands deep in his pockets as he sank into a moody silence. He'd hate himself for hurting Darcy should Darcy find out his primary *and* secondary purpose for asking him out, but if Darcy were in any danger or if he somehow—unwittingly—posed any danger to everyone else, Arlen was left with no other choice.

Well, back then, when he was alone with Darcy, he felt as though he didn't have any other choice. He shouldn't have allowed panic to take over, and he kicked himself for that miserable slip. Why he'd let himself be so affected by someone he barely knew, he couldn't say. But he did, and now he was set to have a date with Darcy Winter, whose heart was doomed to be broken once everything was over and done with.

How would one fix that kind of a fallout?

Was it even possible to rectify it? Arlen had to sigh, shoulders slumping.

"Come on, let's go check out the cemetery," Gloria piped up after a moment. She nudged Arlen playfully. "Darcy's at work, it's still daytime, and we're done with our jobs. You going hunting tonight after your date?"

"Maybe. Depends on when—yeah. I guess I am."

Arlen would have to, anyway, to keep his mind off the inevitable disaster he'd just set up for himself. The pair finished taking a turn around the Institute's quad, and they were soon in Gloria's car, heading out in St. Anthony's direction.

* * * *

Arlen could see where someone had recently trimmed—or attempted to trim—some of the overgrowth that was practically burying the sad little cemetery under so much weight. The work was patchy at best, clearly showing the efforts of one person, most likely someone who didn't have the right sort of tools and equipment to get things done properly. It was the work of a disadvantaged amateur, but the efforts were, indeed, laudable.

They were also quite touching.

Why, after all, would anyone attempt such a monumental job with no help?

Arlen stood in knee-high grass and weeds, his hands on his hips as he gazed around him. Somewhere in the cemetery, Gloria trudged and read, and he could hear her movements easily. It was awfully quiet in that area, he thought. Perhaps too quiet.

He frowned as he closed his eyes, bowed his head, and focused. His senses sharpened, his magic stirring in his veins as he sought out echoes of past lives in that decrepit old cemetery.

Nothing.

Arlen opened his eyes and moved himself to another part, a random spot close to the more densely wooded area and the outer fringes of what had once been a sprawling forest. St. Anthony's stretched into the shade, about a third of its graves lost in shadows. In the mid-afternoon sun, there was a moodiness to the cover of branches and leaves overhead.

"Weird," Arlen muttered as he focused his senses and his magic again. "I don't—there's nothing here."

"Hey, Arlen?" Gloria called from where she was. "Where the hell are you?"

"In the trees!" he yelled back, shrinking instinctively as the shrillness of his voice in the hollow silence tore at his ears. "Yikes," he muttered, shaking his head as he turned around and picked his way back.

The pair eventually met somewhere near the middle of the cemetery. Arlen took note of the weathered old vault standing in near-ruined pride on his left. Gloria appeared a touch troubled when she finally joined him there.

"What did you get?" she asked.

"Nothing. Not a single damned thing. You?"

"Same. Dude, this is beyond weird. There's no sign of—anything. No residual energies, no echoes, nothing. It's like…"

Arlen rubbed the back of his neck as he gazed around them. "It's like St. Anthony's a dead cemetery. Literally."

And yet, he couldn't help but note, there was something—or there seemed to be something—lurking ever so faintly somewhere just outside the reach of his magic and his enhanced senses. He couldn't say what it was, couldn't even determine if it posed a threat or if it was nothing more than a benign shadow of the cemetery's slumbering residents. It felt more like an echo of an echo, a whisper of a whisper.

There should be easily read imprints everywhere, he decided, frowning. But they were simply subdued—forced into a near-silent state. Muffled by something strong enough for its influence to remain effective. Why the extreme suppression, though? Magic surely had something to do with St. Anthony's muteness, but why deny the dead their existence? Why silence their long-gone lives as though they never existed at one point?

Arlen had once studied a strange case from the mid-19th century involving an island city in Italy, where an old cemetery had been drained of its sleepers' residual imprints. And it was all because of a plague of revenants and the blackened soul of a dead aristocrat—all those together worked to drain the cemetery of its echoes in order to sustain their unnatural power.

One of the vampire hunters who'd lived there and had moved to England once the scourge was eliminated had written scholarly tracts on Italy's more terrifying kind of magic. Those books had since become required reading for future generations of sorcerer-hunters, and Arlen remembered being horrified and deeply fascinated with Michele De Santis's accounts.

So was something similar happening to St. Anthony's? Arlen shuddered to think.

"What do you think it means, though?" Gloria prodded, turning her attention to the nearest gravestone and crouching next to it. She took a moment to read and decipher the barely legible carvings on the discolored and weathered stone. "Man. This is too sad. This person doesn't even have a name anymore."

"I know. All of the gravestones are like that."

Lives long gone, permanently erased from memory. From knowledge. What a terrible fate for the dead, to be forgotten completely, with no one left—not even descendants, if there were any—to acknowledge their existence. Arlen's rambling thoughts settled on the recently trimmed vines and weeds of a nearby section of the cemetery. No, not completely forgotten, he amended, a brow rising in some admiration and surprise. Someone had been trying to take care of St. Anthony's, ensuring the dead were accorded the respect they deserve.

"Darcy must have done this," he said, resting his hands on his hips again. When Gloria met his gaze questioningly, he nodded at the trimmed area. "He must be coming here now and then to clear out the overgrowth. See that spot?"

"Yeah. Wow. If that's true, maybe that's the reason behind the weird readings we've been getting from him."

Arlen frowned. "You think so? I guess that makes sense."

That, of course, didn't mean he could just up and break off the date, he told himself. If Gloria's guess proved to be fact, there was still that strange bit about St. Anthony's being quite—dead. All cemeteries, regardless of age, kept a certain amount of psychic imprints from those buried there. It was simply Nature's way of allowing mortals to leave a faint mark of some kind once the spirit crossed into the world of the dead.

A human life's connection to its past was a guarantee, allowing survivors a chance to grieve, to accept, to embrace, and to celebrate. It was a cycle, the bittersweet nature of a mortal's fragile and short existence finding some form of immortality in its much, much quieter echoes.

Good or bad, regardless of a person's nature or how they lived their lives, such things simply were. Magic-wielders through the centuries had always said, "It's the way of things as Nature intended."

But for a cemetery where a dozen bodies—thirteen if one were to consider the vault—were buried or interred—for such a place to exhibit nothing but an unnerving kind of silence—Arlen knew it boded ill.

"Wait," Gloria hissed suddenly, drawing him from his thoughts. "What was that?"

"Huh? What?"

Gloria held up a hand to silence him, and she stilled, her figure stiff as she strained her ears to listen. At length she shook her head and sighed, dropping her hand. "Nothing. I guess it's true what they say about dead silence making you hallucinate."

Arlen blew out a breath. "We'd better go. I think this place is starting to get under our skin even with the sun up like this."

"I'm hungry. Are you in the mood for a burger?"

Arlen grinned and slapped a hand against his friend's shoulder as they turned toward the gate. "Dude, I'm *always* in the mood for a burger. As long as you're buying."

"Asshole."

The two turned around and clumsily picked their way through the forest of vines, weeds, and gravestones toward the cemetery gate.

"Hey, remember that book about vampires in Italy from way back? Like, over a century ago?"

Gloria didn't answer right away. "Oh, yeah. That was pretty intense reading. I did my dissertation on revenants, you know."

"Really? Well—I'm wondering now if what's happening to St. Anthony's is related to that."

"Vampires in Dolores, dude? Really?"

Arlen chuckled as he forced the gate apart with some effort, allowing Gloria to stumble through before he followed her. No, revenants might not be possible, but toying with the possibility gave Arlen's thoughts a much-needed boost, which, in turn, fed his guilt-ridden desire to wheedle as much information as he could from Darcy.

Chapter 7

Darcy was overdressed for work, and he knew it. It was embarrassing, to say the least, and it sure didn't help that Benjamin and Zoe appeared to know what was up. What made things even more mortifying was the fact that neither of the two said a word about Darcy's clothes, the conspiratorial twinkle in their eyes doing a good enough job of telling him what was on their minds.

His brain was a mess. And it certainly didn't help that he'd had a pretty restless night, unsettling dreams he couldn't even recall upon awakening pulling him out of sleep a number of times till his alarm rang. Distracted and confused, Darcy went about his day fumbling and making the smallest and dumbest mistakes. He was red-faced and stammering apologies left and right, though it seemed as if customers didn't know what it was he was sorry for, while everything appeared to be going wrong for him in his mind.

He'd received a reassuring pat on the hand from at least three little old ladies who cooed, "There, there, honey—everything's going to be just fine."

By the time his shift ended, he absolutely had no idea what happened from the moment he woke up. Once or twice—all right, he had to admit to himself, *thrice* at minimum—he'd considered sidling up to his companions to ask for advice.

"I'm going to screw things up," he hissed once he found a moment to breathe in between customer traffic. He glanced up at Benjamin, who merely regarded him with a somewhat pitying look on his face. "It's my first ever date. How do I keep myself from making a total dumpster fire of things, Ben?"

"Dude, it's going to be okay. Seriously. Don't try too hard to impress him. He asked you for a date because he likes you, all right?"

"I'm a better listener than I am a talker," Darcy stammered, face burning. "I guess I can always let him lead and then see where things go. Though—I really would rather just listen to him talk and shut up the whole time."

"I don't think that's how dates go, man."

So much for getting some much-needed pep talk, let alone sage advice. Benjamin, moreover, couldn't help him more because the next and final wave of customers, which tended to be the biggest and most frenetic one of the day, arrived. They wouldn't have another chance to talk before the shop closed, and that was simply that. For better or for worse, time also flew along till closing time was called, much to Darcy's dismay. He tried to distract himself with final cleaning duties.

Darcy was wiping down the counter when Benjamin walked up to him and gently slapped his shoulder.

"Go, man," Benjamin said, his low voice a throaty rumble. "Go on and enjoy."

Darcy barely had a chance to say anything back because the door opened at that moment, and in stepped Arlen—resplendent as ever in his usual black suit. Did the man ever wear anything else? Darcy blinked. Did Arlen wear a business suit to his night hunts? Well, that would have to be one subject he could raise in conversation, at least.

"Hey," Arlen said, his voice soft and tentative—uncertain. Even his smile seemed uncertain as he approached the counter. "You ready?"

Darcy swallowed and glanced over to Benjamin, who stood just behind him. "I haven't—"

"I'll clock you out. Don't worry. Go and have fun," Benjamin replied. He seemed like an older brother at that moment, the way he fussed over Darcy. Then he turned his attention to Arlen and quickly stepped around Darcy, beckoning to his friend for what appeared to be a quiet chat.

Darcy hurried to the back to dispose of the rag and wash his hands. A quick check of the staff room revealed nothing of his left behind, so he scurried back out, a pitiful bag of nerves. Benjamin and Arlen were still having a hushed conversation by the door, and Zoe gave Darcy a wink and a thumbs up as he trotted past her.

"Good luck breaking that one in," she whispered.

"Th—thank you."

Benjamin glanced back and grinned at Darcy as he neared the two. "All right. Have fun, kids."

Benjamin had an arm around Arlen's shoulders, and he gave them one final squeeze before releasing his friend and letting Arlen move toward Darcy. Whatever it was the two talked about, it must have been pretty intense. Arlen's complexion was red, and his eyes looked a touch wild. Benjamin, on the other hand, simply ambled back to the counter, hands in pockets as he whistled.

Darcy didn't have time to wonder about anything. Arlen opened the door for him and smiled, the earlier look of panic—was it panic?—now finally gone and replaced with the easy smile Darcy was so used to seeing on him.

As they walked out into the early evening scene of downtown, Darcy said, "I hope Benjamin didn't just mess with your head."

"Let's just say both heads are kind of on the line if I fuck things up tonight."

Big brothers, Darcy thought, sighing. Couldn't get away from them even in surrogate form.

"Sorry. He can be kind of protective."

Arlen merely chuckled, taking Darcy's arm in a gentle hold while guiding him down the brightly lit boulevard. Darcy noticed they were moving in the general direction of his cabin, which probably meant Arlen wanted to ensure Darcy's ease and sense of safety and comfort by bringing him closer to home. A warmth suffused Darcy's cheeks as the weight of the moment slowly sank in, and disbelief refused to give up the fight.

Arlen Stroescu, gorgeous sorcerer-hunter and overall badass, was taking him out on a date.

Him! Darcy Winter, who never knew his father, lived in a tiny cabin inherited from his mother, boasted only one skill (the cello) and wasn't even that good at it if he were honest about it, and was forced into a penny-pinching lifestyle in order to make sure his monetary inheritance (a massive one, for which he'd referred to himself as a working trust fund baby) lasted for as long as possible. He'd been scouring around for a second part-time job to take up the other two days he was free, having developed an intense paranoia about the state of his fortune throughout his lifetime. He lived in California, after all. The state's minimal requirements for survival could easily threaten a trust fund baby's coffers as far as he saw.

Above all, however, was the awful loneliness often suffocating him whenever he was at home on his weekends. He'd once believed he could manage after his mother passed away, but the longer he lived like this, the more insidious the gnawing feeling of desolation grew. A second job should take care of that dilemma, he thought.

With an internal sigh, Darcy nudged his glasses up and fought off the inevitably growing doubts.

"So, um, where are we going?" he asked, grimacing at how meek he sounded. That Arlen managed to hear him despite the noise of the downtown shopping strip was a damned miracle.

"I'm taking you to my favorite Vietnamese restaurant. Have you had Vietnamese food before? No? Okay, I'll help you find something good on the menu to try out."

The restaurant Arlen took Darcy to was a small family-run hole-in-the-wall type tucked away in one of the smaller side streets about three or so blocks from Benjamin's chocolate shop. A baby-faced young man greeted Arlen with a familiarity that made Darcy's stomach plunge as though a gigantic brick had just been thrown into it.

The host, Thao Trang, led them to a corner booth, handing them a pair of menus and taking their orders for drinks. Darcy, already a bit self-conscious, couldn't help but notice the way Thao eyed Arlen appreciatively, his dark, expressive eyes raking up and down Arlen's person with a deliberate slowness that possibly was meant to be noticed. Not by Arlen, no, but by Darcy.

Darcy deflated a little but held on, turning his attention fully to his drink and then to their dinner once Thao returned with the dishes.

Small talk creaked and groaned forward—like rusty gears only recently oiled, and only barely at that, but it was better than the uncomfortable silence that at first pervaded. Darcy now realized both of them were quite terrible in intimate settings and that nobody had the right kind of skill to pull off a successful first date.

Fits and starts—much of the conversation fell under that category while the pair waited for their meal.

Then Darcy was obligated to ask Arlen about his work, which he already knew a little about, thanks to Benjamin. That somehow segued into Darcy's work, which wasn't much, and then his past. His family. His home.

"I never knew my dad," he said, shrugging weakly before taking another appreciative sip of his hot tea. "I mean—my mom was a single mother, you know? She and my dad never married, and she didn't seem to care too much about that. She taught music at the local high school and also offered private music lessons on the side to keep us going." Darcy refused to mention anything about his remarkable inheritance.

"She was the one who taught you music, then?"

Darcy paused, blinking and cocking his head in some confusion. "How'd you know that?"

"Ah. No, it's—kind of common sense, though, right?" Arlen replied hastily. "If one of your parents is good in, say, music or art or a sport, it pretty much stands to reason that the kid would be given lessons. Do you, uh, play? The cello, I mean? Or other instrument?"

"Yeah. Not very good, but..." Darcy caught himself. He almost blurted something out about the mothers. "I—I guess I'm okay. I do try to practice whenever I can." That much was true, anyway. "I know what you mean about parents teaching their kids the same skills and all that."

Sometimes forced lessons, Darcy appended, but he admitted his proficiency in the cello was because of a desire to learn. His mother had never forced it on him, and it had been Darcy who'd begged to be taught. Arlen nodded, listening with a surprising amount of interest. Perhaps Darcy's doubts were unfounded, after all, and a wave of pleasure—however vaguely shocked—coursed through him, and he couldn't suppress a smile.

"You have a really beautiful smile."

"Oh. Thank you."

"I'll bet you look a lot like your mom. She must've been gorgeous," Arlen said.

"She was, but I can't really say who I look like the most. I don't even have a picture of my dad anywhere."

Arlen fell silent for a moment, concentrating on his food, though a faint crease between his brows told Darcy he was thinking a tad too deeply. Finally he looked up and offered Darcy a small smile.

"What about your cabin? Did you inherit that from your mom?"

Of course, the cabin, Darcy thought, and he laughed softly. Yes, the cabin was his mother's. Yes, she'd also inherited it from her family—her great-grandparents, in fact, because her parents had moved away before she was born. She'd been vague about that point, the reason behind their decision to leave even though every generation before them—specifically her father's side—lived in that same cabin through decade after decade. Her parents had broken the chain, apparently, but Fortune had different ideas in store for the family altogether.

Once she was pregnant with Darcy, she'd received the message about the cabin being a part of her family's legacy. It had taken the lawyers, with the help of a private investigator, in fact, a good length of time, tracking the woman down, and she'd gladly moved to Dolores. She'd taken to the cabin quite easily, by all accounts.

"It's kind of bizarre to have something more like a mountain cabin just right there, outside the city but still part of it," Darcy said, shrugging again. "I grew up in it and am used to it, so I'm good. It's pretty quiet out there, and I've never felt threatened or anything. Never got attacked or robbed. Well—knock on wood, right?"

He rapped on the wall behind him, drawing a cheery laugh from his date.

"What about the cemetery?" Arlen prodded after another moment's silence. "Doesn't that freak you out?"

"Oh, St. Anthony's? Nah. I'm used to having it just down the road from me."

"Have you checked it out, then?" Arlen pursued, his voice shifting ever so slightly, though Darcy couldn't quite read what lay behind his tone. In the end, Darcy decided he was simply looking for something in nothing.

"Yeah, sure. I sometimes go there to cut down the weeds and stuff. It's—pretty sad, having those graves forgotten and left to fall apart like that. Those used to be real, live people, you know. They don't deserve to be neglected like this, even in death. It's kind of a recent thing for me. I used to ignore it until Mom passed away three years ago."

"Maybe they don't have any descendants left—from the family dying out or just moving away. It happens."

"I know. Still sad, though. I do what I can with the tools I have."

When Arlen didn't respond, Darcy glanced up to find his date regarding him with a strange light in his eyes. Admiration? Pleasure? No, it couldn't be. Any decent human being would do exactly what he did for those forgotten dead. Darcy wasn't anything special.

Chapter 8

Arlen looked around, frowning at the darkness. There were no lights anywhere around Darcy's cabin—unsurprisingly, really, given the structure's location. Darcy had told him he pretty much functioned on old-fashioned hexed outlets, which amazed Arlen but then brought him back down to earth upon realizing just how much the service was costing Darcy.

"Is this something your mom and your great-great grandparents set up?" he asked as he escorted Darcy from the car to the cabin's front door.

"Yeah. It's always been like this since I was born, anyway, and I never really bothered to ask Mom about it. Um—it comes in pretty handy if you live way out in the boonies like I do." Darcy appended that with a self-conscious little chuckle, and he ducked his head as he fumbled for his keys.

Hexed outlets certainly worked like solar panels, freeing up their users from any dependence on utility companies, though the magical side of such a service still slapped users with a pricey bill.

"Ah—I wonder if what you have is something like a legacy service. I've heard about those," Arlen said. When Darcy paused and glanced back at him, surprise in his large eyes, Arlen added, "With spells that, you know, help out in day-to-day stuff like electricity or heat, usually there's this clause that allows early users to opt into a legacy deal. If the start-up ends up being successful and keeps going for a long time, those early adopters enjoy a guaranteed service."

"Even when it started with my great-great grandparents?"

"Yeah. That was when the idea originally started, anyway. Even way before. I read about hexed paint from Europe a couple of hundred years ago, for example, and that's pretty much continued to this day. From what I understand, investors back then came from money, and artists who offered to test out the paints were given lifetime supplies of the stuff—even their descendants had them as long as they practiced the same kind of artistic expression or used the same medium as the previous generations. But everyone else who weren't in on the venture from the start obviously had to pay for the privilege of using the stuff to enhance their art."

It really was nothing any different from the modern day counterparts of fund-raising sites for creators and artists who needed extra financial backing to keep their projects going and, in time, officially launched. But when magic was involved, such sites were strictly monitored for potential abuse from users who may have a darker agenda for their fund-raising efforts.

Darcy considered what he'd heard in curious silence. "I guess that makes sense. It's a pretty generous clause if that's the case, isn't it? Is it because it's magic and not science and technology?"

"Well, sure. Stands to reason, anyway, that something that's pretty much defined by the gods would come with some guarantees but also strict rules on how it's used. Like those hexed paints I mentioned. If you buy one as a modern user, you're kind of bound to rules that dictate your use of them."

"I only use the hexed electrical outlets for basic stuff. I should be in the clear," Darcy piped up, grinning, before he went back to getting the front door unlocked. "And, to be honest, the power isn't that strong. You can tell it's totally old-fashioned and goes way, way back."

The moonlight helped, of course, with that being a clear night as well. With the autumn and winter coming sooner than later, Arlen wondered how Darcy managed through the cold. Even hexed electrical outlets could only stand so much usage in extreme weather, and he'd heard of spotty quality control when it came to wizards who specialized in improving modern comforts.

The car was currently parked in the dirt and patchy grass several yards off the main road. Good thing the terrain was quite flat, and Arlen's vehicle didn't have to navigate over deep ruts and surprise rocks.

The cabin made him think of one of those ancient television shows involving the pioneer days. There wasn't even a single bulb over the cabin's front door. A couple of potted cacti flanked the door, the fading summer days reflected in the cacti's wilting flowers, and Arlen couldn't help a small smile from forming at the thought of Darcy looking after such plants in addition to tending to the cemetery.

Darcy unlocked the front door and stepped inside, flicking a light switch and flooding the interior with soft, warm light. He turned around and squirmed a little, his gaze barely fixing itself on Arlen.

"Did you want to come in?" he asked. "I've—I've got some hot tea and brownies. I made the brownies myself. I know we've already had dessert and all, but I figured, you know, a little extra something won't hurt."

In the soft light of the cabin, a deep blush could still be easily seen as Darcy colored.

"I mean—you don't have to, of course. You might have a hunt to take care of or something. Uh…" Darcy sighed, and his entire body sagged. "Sorry. I don't mean to pressure you. I had a great time, though."

Arlen hadn't planned on coming in at first, having contented himself with a preliminary learning of Darcy's history. He had the data in mind, and he was looking forward to using it while researching the Winter family tree and its possible link to St. Anthony's. But the invitation, however shyly given, also opened a door for him—a chance to look inside Darcy's home and get a full reading of the place.

But Darcy's obvious discomfort and awkwardness in inviting Arlen inside also stirred something in Arlen, a surprising burst of quiet warmth for the young man who appeared to find himself in over his head.

"Sure," he replied, smiling.

Darcy blinked. "Really? Oh. Oh, sorry. Yeah, come on in," he stammered and stepped farther inside to welcome his guest. "I'm not used to having someone over. You're sort of the first person I've ever invited here. Even Mom didn't have visitors."

"Hey, it's cool, really. It's all good."

Darcy entered and waved Arlen in.

And it was a good thing Darcy immediately turned his attention to making his home comfortable for his guest because he'd have seen Arlen suck in a breath and stagger a few steps, throwing a hand out to hold himself steady against the nearest wall.

Arlen couldn't breathe. It felt as though something had just punched him in the stomach while an invisible and impossibly thick curtain fell on him, bearing down on him with incredible weight. There was a frightening physicality to the assault on his senses, but he managed to pull himself together with some help from his magic. The invisible curtain gradually dissipated, but its weight continued to push down on him.

For the next moment, he busied himself with a thorough visual examination of the cabin. It allowed him to compose himself again and focus his mind on his surroundings while keeping his magic faintly simmering below the surface. It would be easily roused in a breath.

Darcy's cabin was absolutely tiny, with Arlen mentally calculating square footage to about 700, definitely no more than 750. The front door opened into the main cabin space. On the left was the small sofa, an equally small bookcase, a picture window, and a fireplace on the wall opposite the sofa.

On the right was the combination kitchen and dining area with an old, square, oak table seating two people standing by the significantly larger picture window that looked out into the road. A narrow sideboard and hutch stood against the wall directly across the way from the window.

The kitchen was nothing more than a relatively short tiled counter, small sink, and lower cabinets. A stove whose burners were covered stood at one end of the counter, and the short refrigerator graced the other end. A second door appeared next to the refrigerator, and the corner of that end of the cabin contained the furnace and the washer and dryer.

Behind the living room wall was the bedroom—easily spotted from the front door as the room itself didn't have an actual door, only the doorway. Arlen noted a small window that opened out to the woodland behind the cabin, and the foot of the bed peeked out from the left side, behind the wall.

"There's a small loft upstairs," Darcy offered as he walked to the kitchen. "I call it a garret room because it's sort of like an attic space, but I slept there when Mom was still alive. Now I practice my cello up there whenever I can. If you need to use the bathroom, it's next to the stairs—just right by the washer and dryer."

Darcy proceeded to open the cabinets and dig around for the kettle. Arlen idly walked around, calling on his magic to feel around the cabin. The place was definitely sagging from the weight of the supernatural, though its nature and especially the source remained elusive.

He sauntered over to the washer and dryer and glanced up the dark stairs on his left, the sight of the narrow wooden steps vanishing in deep shadows sending a shiver of unease through him. The second half of the stairs was in utter darkness, raising a myriad of frightening possibilities in Arlen's mind. The mere visual representation of an unlit, narrow stairway terminating in pitch blackness made him think back to childhood nightmares.

He quietly sent out a magical probe of sorts, a ghostly sphere that spun slowly as it ascended and then vanished upstairs. It was going to read the loft for him, communicating its results through a psychic link with its creator before he summoned it back.

The hexed lights in the cabin were quite dim, a yellowish glow that Arlen could compare to an extremely low wattage bulb. This was perhaps the limitation of the hexed lights, at least for those with legacy contracts. Darcy could have bought into a higher quality of illumination, but Arlen figured money was a huge issue for the young man. He'd just learned that Darcy had been seeking out a second part-time job, and Arlen grimaced at the thought. That was simply too much, too soon, for someone who was just starting out in life.

With the hexed lights, Arlen wondered if Darcy's great-great-grandparents were wealthy. For such a service to continue through over a century, surely a good deal of money had been invested. It was just too bad the newest owner of the rustic little cabin didn't enjoy much else but the most basic necessities. Money certainly had a strange way of disappearing, and Arlen wished Darcy's inheritance had been much more than just the cabin. He certainly deserved it.

Sudden guilt surged through Arlen at his idle musings. He was jumping to conclusions without anything solid to go by. What would he really know about Darcy's financial situation and especially his connection to the cabin? For all he knew, Darcy absolutely loved living there, quietly sequestered from the hubbub of the city.

"I'd love to hear you play your music sometime," Arlen said after clearing his throat.

He turned around and walked back to the dining table, where Darcy had set a couple of chipped dessert plates and forks. To Arlen's amusement, his young host had also set down dainty cups and saucers—mismatched, at that—by the plates. In the middle of the table sat a platter of brownies.

"I didn't know you like classical music."

"I like a lot of music, really, though I need to expose myself to more classical stuff."

Once the kettle whistled, Darcy poured them hot water and slid a small box of teabags toward Arlen. The pair settled down to enjoy a post-date repast, with conversation again falling into a quiet and comfortable rhythm. The dim light felt surprisingly relaxing, easing Arlen's mind and allowing him to forget everything about his purpose in asking Darcy out.

The scene was also quite domestic, catching him by surprise, but he quickly discovered how much he liked it. It was a far, far cry from the dangerous activities he and his peers took to at night, usually closer to midnight at that, flying overhead from building to building in the city proper, chasing after restless spirits and sending them back with the help of their goddess, Hecate, and her ghostly hounds.

What he now enjoyed in Darcy's company was almost jarring in its simplicity and its celebration of the most basic things. Brownie after brownie, refill after refill, the conversation went on for an hour or so. The two of them talked about everything and nothing, their exchange breaking up with occasional laughter or exclamations of shock, dismay, and even anger.

But perhaps what made Arlen lose himself in even greater wonder was the glowing, sweetly smiling face of his host as Darcy talked and opened up to Arlen with the guilelessness of a child. Never in Arlen's life had he been given a chance to really watch how a hundred different emotions could so easily make themselves known in the human face, though in Darcy's case, this vulnerability seemed to make him breathlessly beautiful.

Chapter 9

Dolores's main cemetery always threw Darcy off his center whenever he came by to visit. Once a month, every month since his mother's passing from cancer just after his eighteenth birthday, Darcy had stopped by with a small collection of flowers.

It was a vast, beautifully sprawling cemetery, the entire place divided into four sections. His mother was buried in The Meadows, which was the quadrant located the farthest from the road and the cemetery's busier mausoleum and outdoor graveyard.

The Meadows was also one of the pricier choices, but Darcy had made sure to spend as much as he could for the woman whom he loved above all else.

Charlotte Winter was a quiet, even-tempered, and shy woman in life, and her absolute passion for music and her only child were things Darcy made sure to honor for as long as he breathed. She was retiring and enjoyed silent and calming vistas, where she'd always take Darcy for picnics or for simple walks and conversation. It was only right that she'd be allowed such things in death as well.

"Hi, Mom," Darcy said after setting the flowers on the headstone and touching her name with his fingers. He sat down on the perfectly trimmed grass, legs crossed under him. "I, um, I had a date with someone I really like. Pretty weird, I know, but I never thought he'd be interested in me enough to want to have dinner with me. I gave him some of the brownies I made from your recipe book at home, but—nothing really happened after."

It was just a surprisingly lovely end to a very enjoyable date despite the earlier discomfort of having someone else blatantly show appreciation and even a hint of challenge over Arlen. Of course, Darcy berated himself, who wouldn't want to challenge some gangly, four-eyed upstart over Arlen Stroescu?

He sighed and dropped his gaze to the grass and his fingers as he now absentmindedly brushed the lush growth as though stroking a favorite pet.

He quietly talked about their dinner at the Vietnamese restaurant, the nice, idle saunter around downtown Dolores, which was a hive of light, color, activity, and amazing energy. Things, in brief, Darcy wasn't so used to, and had at first left him overwhelmed and speechless from confusion.

But Arlen had taken good care of him the whole time, whether or not the young man was even aware of what he was doing then. Darcy basked in the memory of Arlen's presence beside him, the occasional brushing of their arms and the even more frequent holding of Darcy's elbow whenever Arlen needed to steer him somewhere.

Usually away from a crush of shoppers and nightlife enthusiasts.

Darcy had always gone straight home from work, driven home by either Zoe—who lived in the small town next to Dolores—or Benjamin, who refused to see Darcy brave the lonely rural road leading out of the city at night. Not once had he felt any interest in what happened around Dolores after the chocolate shop closed at 6 pm. He might have a pretty good idea based on what he usually saw during the day, but suddenly finding himself in the thick of things proved to be a bit of a shock.

But Arlen…

Darcy smiled, feeling the familiar warmth suffuse his face as he avoided looking up at the headstone, mentally replaying Arlen's solicitousness and un-wavering attention.

"He asked me a lot about our family, too, Mom," he said after he finished his account. This time he looked up and ran his gaze over his mother's name and the stylized image of the weeping willow carved beneath it. "I never expected him to be so keen on learning more about us—about you and grandpa, grand-ma, and even my great-grandparents and everyone else who came before them."

He shrugged. "I wish I showed as much interest in his own history," he said, his voice dropping to an embarrassed half-whisper. "I feel pretty badly about that, so maybe—maybe if he were to ask me out on another date, it'll be my turn to know more about him."

Darcy sighed and relaxed, this time glancing up and watching the bright open skies above and wondering if his mother actually heard him. He hoped, anyway.

"Oh—I'm thinking of working a second job, so I won't be visiting you on a regular basis. I'm sorry, Mom. I can always move out, but I—I can't just leave our home. Who'll look after the mothers if I go? We've always done it, right? It shouldn't end like this. I mean, they deserve way better, just like you said."

There was also the matter of the cabin and whether or not it should be sold to someone else. A wave of jealousy and protectiveness swept over Darcy at the thought, particularly when it came to St. Anthony's. If someone else did buy the cabin from him, would they give a damn about the cemetery down the road? Most likely St. Anthony's would be forgotten and surrendered to Nature.

At worst? Decimated and completely flattened by bulldozer as it would likely be considered an eyesore. Unless, of course, the new owners happened to be overly superstitious and quite gullible to suggestions of bad luck and other things. Then the flattened space that was once St. Anthony's would also be blessed twenty times over to keep evil influences away. No, Darcy thought, resolve deepening. No, he would never leave his home. He knew better. The mothers deserved better.

He never said a word about the mothers to Arlen the previous night. He was honor-bound to keep his occasional care a secret. It wasn't any different from when his own mother had looked after those poor women, and while she never spoke of it overtly, she'd managed to drop a hint here and there about her predecessors somehow learning something about the mothers and St. Anthony's history from an old diary or a collection of letters she'd read.

Nothing came of it, of course, as Darcy had been too young and too wrapped up in school then. But she'd certainly taken great care in emphasizing the importance of her role as a mother who offered solace to others like her.

Others like her.

Darcy stopped and considered that point. It was a brief reminder of a comment she'd made only fleetingly and even dismissively. How odd that it would somehow come to the fore now, when he no longer had the means of asking for an explanation.

Others like her, he thought, frowning a little. A single mother, perhaps? Were the mothers also unmarried before they died? Darcy might have to try to dig around for more information about St. Anthony's. If Arlen and Gloria and their cohorts in the Institute of Arcane Studies would allow him, he'd ask for their help in some research.

The cemetery itself wasn't any help. All of the gravestones were in such bad shape that even the names of the dead had been obliterated by time and the elements. Even the solitary vault in the middle of the burial ground had no name anywhere. If a plaque had once identified the vault's occupant (or occupants), it had long vanished.

He'd have to sort out a plan of action once he returned home.

Darcy spent perhaps close to an hour in the cemetery, turning to a book he'd brought with him after he finished updating his mother with his day-to-day life. The book was another comforting activity, one that recalled the past and brought him back to those days when he and his mother spent entire afternoons or whatever free time she had reading together. He had his preferences, and she had hers.

They'd bring their books with them to wherever they decided to spend time in quiet enjoyment of the great outdoors. Or they'd simply hang around in the cabin together, lost in their tomes while the old clock ticked away, and quiet music played from the CD player.

Before long Darcy was riding the bus back to one of the outermost edges of the city, and there he'd alight then walk the rest of the way home.

* * * *

"I wish you could tell me who you are," Darcy said after the final notes of the music faded gently into the night. He moved his gaze from one expressionless skull to another. "I wish I knew your stories, so I could honor you better. I can only do so much for you like this."

The mothers merely squeaked and clicked, shifting where they lay, sat, or stood. Dry bones rubbed and scraped against the floorboards, with earth and dust rising from where rotten fabric and even hair moved. Darcy had just performed a lively and darkly dramatic piece, one which he'd fallen in love with when he'd first heard it interpreted by a five-piece cello ensemble: Schubert's *Erlkönig*.

He'd long been familiar with the ballad by Goethe, the terrifying imagery of a father fleeing unnatural, primeval forces in a vain hope of saving his child searing itself in his brain. And to hear Schubert's musical interpretation of it arranged for the cello turned into a siren's call to Darcy.

There was something about the dark ballad that had found its roots deep in him. That somehow, incomprehensibly at that, he felt he was closely linked to the story. His mother hadn't once said anything that gave him such a bizarre and fanciful idea, but there was simply something about the connection between his life and a poem written centuries ago that he couldn't shake off, let alone dismiss off-hand.

And the mothers had responded to the piece.

He'd already played it three times, but their movements and the general air in the garret room convinced him he couldn't—shouldn't—move on to the next piece he had in mind for that evening's performance.

There was a singular restlessness to their movements. If they were alive, Darcy could imagine them squirming in their seats, exchanging meaningful glances before pleading for him to play again. In fact, a couple of them had tried to inch forward, raising their skeletal arms and reaching out to him. A third had opened both of her arms as though asking for an embrace.

"If only you could talk," he said, sighing.

When nothing but the usual wheezing and vague squawks met his ears, he set his bow against the strings again and started over.

He was about a third of the way done when a sound brought everything to a halt.

A frantic knocking. The sound of something furiously rapping against the cabin wall from outside. Or was it the side door? It was difficult to make out at first, the sounds more felt than heard, given their oddly muted quality.

Darcy looked around and quickly stood up, while the mothers skittered backward, their movements now a great deal more alarmed. They were also faster in the way they vanished into the shadows, their squeaks, clicks, and wheezes rising in volume and making Darcy think of panicking animals. Those on their bellies crawled backward, those who limped or hobbled into view turned around and hurried back, a group of corpses pushing and shoving their way out of the garret. Like a startled stampede of the dead, Darcy thought, and he set his cello aside before hurrying down the narrow stairs.

He stood in the kitchen area, his gaze darting everywhere as he tried to determine where the knocking was really coming from. Even then, when he was closer to the sounds, they remained quiet and distant despite their apparent desperation.

"What the hell?" he breathed.

He'd long drawn the curtains, so there was no way he could see what it was that continued to knock against the cabin walls. It moved as well, whatever it was. It struck the wall behind the refrigerator and then it did it again behind the stove. Then it moved to the front door and knocked repeatedly yet quietly. After a few seconds of that, the night fell eerily silent.

Chapter 10

Arlen bowed his head in reverence before sinking to one knee and pressing a hand on the very spot where the ghost he'd just dispatched vanished. Around him Hecate's phantom hounds snuffled and paced, though he could see none of the dogs. He felt them, though, as was the usual case when sorcerer-hunters went out into the night, guided and led by the immortal pack of the goddess of the crossroads.

"Be at peace, friend," he whispered before launching into a brief and quiet blessing for the poor ghost's eternal rest.

He stood up after another moment, regret and grief in his heart even as the invisible hounds yipped almost playfully at him. It was perhaps the hardest thing for him to do as a sorcerer-hunter: cornering and forcing a restless spirit across the veil. He'd sent too many of them away already, and it pained him to know there were so many deceased out there who held on to mortal life so desperately.

It was unfair, for instance, for this ghost—a boy of about fourteen—to have died at such an age from a car accident. But Fortune kept her cards close, and not even the most powerful sorcerer who ever lived could peer into her heart.

Arlen glanced around him, listening to the hounds as they awaited his command.

"Go now," he said in as soothing and gentle a voice as he could manage. He sighed and ran a shaking hand through his hair. "And rest with your mistress. You've done your job tonight, and you've done it well."

A howl rose—one dog—which was immediately picked up and echoed by another and then another till the entire pack, it seemed, rent the night with their mournful cries. Then they ran off in a rush of icy winds, answering the goddess's summons and quite likely eager to be rewarded for another task fulfilled. A lost, confused, and terrified soul had been collected and guided back to its rightful world, where there it would find all the peace, joy, and solace the world of the dead could offer.

Arlen now stood on the rooftop of an old, abandoned warehouse in the far northern part of Dolores. As he gazed across the sea of roofs and chimneys, he could spot another sorcerer-hunter leaping in high arcs from one rooftop to another. There were usually about seven of them actively pursuing ghosts at any given night, depending on what the oracle tells them. Earlier that day, Coeus's quill had been wildly active, scribbling line after line alerting Arlen to the possible level of supernatural activity that evening.

He took in a deep breath to compose himself, his mind already wandering to a late night pizza trip to his favorite giant-slice pizza shop just five blocks away. Hunting took a great deal out of a sorcerer, the use of magic brought up to just about the maximum level.

"Yep. A ginormous, fat pizza slice sounds perfect right now," he muttered. "Hooray for twenty-four-hour, cheap-ass pizza joints."

He called for his magic and then ran, kicking off the edge of the rooftop and launching himself into the air. He flew through the night air, enjoying the rush of cool wind against his face. Before long he was walking along the street catering to cash-strapped college students, hence the abundance of twenty-four-hour cheap food joints.

He ordered his pepperoni slice and large drink, and he took a spot against the wall. A long table that looked more like a shelf had been secured to that wall, and there hungry customers ate their food, standing and roughing it up, in a way. Arlen loved it.

As he ate, he thought about Darcy and their date. A fond little smile broke through, and while he'd normally be mulling over the questions regarding Darcy's history and his connection to the cemetery, Arlen found he couldn't. Maybe it was because of the hunt. Maybe it was the decadent indulgence of a massive slice of fattening, cheap pizza. Whatever the reason, he couldn't think—refused to think—about his purpose for asking Darcy out on a date in the first place.

He found Darcy Winter to be a bit of a cipher, albeit a good one. The young man was open—perhaps too open, in Arlen's rather jaded opinion. Darcy was surely setting himself up, however unwittingly, for a world of pain. And he wasn't a teenager anymore. For him to go about his days with the same wide-eyed sweetness was...

Well, it was too much for Arlen to bear in a way. He didn't like the idea. He felt...

Protective.

Arlen blinked and paused, mid-chew. Surely that was just a natural response to Darcy's clear naïveté. Who wouldn't feel the same way? Darcy was pretty potent in his own way, his influence on people quite impressive, and Arlen had seen the results. Benjamin, who'd only known Darcy since Darcy's hire date, threatened to rip Arlen's genitals out if he hurt his date in any way. Gloria, who was very much just as obsessive about work as Arlen was, had also shown a few chinks in her armor when it came to Darcy.

Don't break his heart.

Arlen sighed and shook off the sudden and uncomfortable wave of maudlin thoughts. No, he shouldn't lose sight of the possible dangers Darcy may pose. The cabin nearly knocked him over the moment he stepped inside, the lingering effects of otherworldly essences bearing down on him from every corner. In fact, it seemed as though every inch of wood, paint, paper, and glass making up the cabin had been thoroughly soaked in the supernatural.

And poor Darcy, having grown up in such a place, had understandably been cloaked in the stuff.

Arlen finished his meal and left, idea after idea careening madly around in his skull as he moved through the now thinner midnight crowd of that part of Dolores. He needed to go somewhere and call back the magical probe he'd let loose in the cabin the previous night. He ought to leave it there for a week if he wished to get a more thorough picture of what was happening in the cabin, but a very insistent gut feeling urged him to do it now.

He eventually found himself in a tiny park right in front of city hall, and it took him a moment to find a bench unoccupied by a homeless unfortunate. There he settled himself, made sure no one else was watching him, and closed his eyes to focus and draw on his magic.

"Come," he whispered. "Tell me what you found."

It took a few seconds before the link came alive, and Arlen's senses felt as though they'd just had their settings pushed to overdrive. His eyes flew open, and he doubled over with a ragged cry.

* * * *

"Darcy! Darcy!"

He knew it was utterly ridiculous, calling Darcy's name in a blind panic, because he was still sailing between rooftops and leaping from spot to spot. But he couldn't help it, the rough image formed in his mind from the psychic connection with his magical probe urging him on.

He didn't even know at the moment if the image was a literal one or something representative of what haunted Darcy's steps. All he knew was the fact that Darcy was surrounded—overcome—by ghosts. Reaching out to him, holding out rotting arms and beckoning to him, crawling and hobbling closer and closer. There was also one more figure, more horrifying than the others. A leader, almost, at least from what Arlen could gather.

As he bounded from one rooftop to another, the terrifying form kept its hold on his mind.

In his vision, it was a ghoulish figure of a priest—no, a man in an old discolored cloak and hood, which brought to mind a burial shroud. The hood had been thrown back, however, revealing the man's features, and that was only one part of a terrifying whole. His face was the face of the dead, frozen in a state of half-decay.

The eyelids were closed, the mouth hanging open with the lips gone, the teeth and tongue nearly hanging out. The skin itself was a dreadful white-gray, the hands poking out of the robe's sleeves a vision in shriveled skin and tissue, the fingers gnarled and almost talon-like.

The shroud itself was old and threadbare, tattered and torn in several places, its lower half a ragged mess of barely held together strips of dried cloth. What it exposed, however, made Arlen's blood ran cold.

Instead of legs and feet, the man seemed to move about on five skeletal fingers. Thumb, index finger, middle finger, ring finger, and pinky—all five digits looked as though they were all part of a giant, otherworldly hand serving the purpose of legs and feet. What was even more ghoulish was the fact that the fingers still exhibited bits of white-gray skin—shrunken and mummified skin, in a way—covering a number of parts as though, like the rest of the monstrosity, the hand had been frozen in a state of partial decay.

The corpse, whatever it was, staggered out of the gray and icy mists of the world of the dead, its horrific and ghastly figure slowly taking shape and revealing itself to the probe. It was the leader of a phantom pack surrounding Darcy and edging closer and closer. Arlen didn't know where it was, whether or not it was inside the cabin with Darcy. But he knew it was there. Or at the very least, it was close—close enough to be a threat.

"Darcy!" he cried.

The last of the shops and houses soon gave way to the open road and the dark fields and the woodland carpeting the final boundaries of Dolores. From the great height he was now sailing earthbound from, Arlen could see the moon-kissed shape of Darcy's modest little cabin.

"Darcy! I'm coming!"

Something tugged at Arlen's magic as he drew closer. Something old but strong, and it gave off a fetid odor. Nothing could be seen lurking about the cabin, and with a frantic whispered spell, Arlen flung both hands out and threw a bolt of illuminating energy.

Not an ordinary light, by any stretch, but one only sorcerers could see because it worked on a level much, much too subtle for the ordinary and untrained human eye. It was also psychically linked to its caster, and with a gasp of horror, Arlen saw the surrounding area of Darcy's cabin glowing in a yellow-green hue, the midnight shadows shrinking away as though in fear.

All except one.

A shadow, yes, but one that was twisted and misshapen, lurking about the front door. Arlen recognized its form easily enough as it raised a hand and knocked on the wood, its movements jerky and uncoordinated. The movements of a reanimated corpse.

And even from where he was, rapidly closing in and feeling a stitch on his side as he fought to speed up, Arlen could still see the terrible oversized, partially decayed phalanges peeking out from its torn robes. When it moved, it skittered, its finger-legs working like the legs of a spider. Arlen shouted again, and the creature immediately turned, saw him, and then raised an arm, fingers pointed.

Arlen nearly skidded to a halt in confusion as he watched the ghost indicate the cemetery. It saw him, to be sure, knew he'd spotted it. But the curious gesture of pointing in the direction of St. Anthony's added to the growing puzzle of its existence.

For a handful of seconds, the world seemed to pause, Arlen and the ghost seemingly at an impasse.

Then the ghost moved, skittering toward the cemetery.

"Damn it," Arlen hissed, leaping into action again, throwing another bolt of illuminating energy out, charging it to encase the phantom and let it lead him to where it wanted him to go.

Much good that did him. The closer they got to St. Anthony's, the more the ghost faded, as though its misty form were being absorbed by the gathering shadows of the cemetery till nothing was left. The illuminating energy then lost its hold and its power, and Arlen was left with an ordinary scene steeped in moonlight.

Chapter 11

"Darcy! I'm coming!"

Darcy blinked as he pressed himself against the wall next to the sideboard. What on earth was that?

"Arlen?" he stammered, his voice weak and thin in his ears.

He gasped at the sudden barrage of sounds that immediately followed. The knocking started again, this time more emphatically as though whoever was outside had grown desperate, though again, the volume remained quite muted. Then it stopped, a momentary pause followed, which in turn preceded a series of wild scuttling sounds as well as a rush of movement through space by another—a second person, apparently. There was a crunch of gravel and loose sand as whatever it was that had been—flying—had just landed on solid ground and now took up the chase on foot.

The sounds moved from the door to the side of the cabin and off, following the road, apparently. Or, Darcy realized, the cemetery.

He dared not move while strange and frantic activity continued somewhere outside. He didn't realize he'd slid down to the floor and had pulled his knees tightly against his chest in a nervous ball. The sounds quickly faded into the night, and within seconds all Darcy could hear was his heavy and ragged breathing.

He allowed himself another few minutes of pathetically cowering in his own home before deeming it safe enough to stand up and move around. The area outside the cabin was, indeed, quiet again, with only the soothing chirps of crickets gently breaking the calm.

He peered into the bedroom and was pleased to see the small window there still secure. The two windows in the garret room were also locked, though perhaps only the one in the bathroom had been pushed up a little to allow steam to leave. Darcy immediately bolted into the kitchen and then skidded to a halt just inside the bathroom, eyes wide as he stared at the window.

Yes, he'd opened it earlier by a couple or more inches, but there was a protective screen that kept bugs and other random critters from entering the cabin. All the same, he knew whatever had just come around to demand entry wasn't any of those. He immediately lunged for the window and pulled it down, turning the latch and testing it repeatedly before feeling an ounce of reassurance.

A quick inspection of the side door showed it just as secured against the outside world, though Darcy couldn't help but eye the two picture windows with a frisson of disquiet. Neither window could be opened, but they were large enough to be easily shattered by something large and heavy thrown against them. The one in the dining room was the largest, and the one in the living room not as much but sizable enough to be cause for worry.

How much would protective hexes cost him? Would they even work?

Darcy walked over to the kitchen counter and carefully pulled back the short curtain covering the narrow, rectangular kitchen window. He peered out, holding his breath, and found nothing but darkness outside. There might be a touch of cloud cover at the moment as the moonlight wasn't flooding the general area or at least touching strategic places that would have allowed him a clearer look of the outside.

Then as though in answer, the clouds seemed to move out of the moon's way, and the area outside was once again cloaked with silver light.

Darcy swallowed and let the curtain drop.

He really needed to go to bed. It was well past his bedtime, and he needed to start off early in the morning for a job interview before heading over to the chocolate shop. With a heavy and exhausted sigh, Darcy checked the locks on the doors again, took care of his bedtime rituals in the bathroom, and then shuffled off to the bedroom, yawning loudly.

He turned the lights off and crawled into bed, his tired gaze straying to the open bedroom door. It had never bothered him in the past that the doorway was never secured with a functional door. He couldn't even remember what had happened to it, but he did suspect it must have been taken out before his mother laid claim to the property.

It took him longer than usual despite his tiredness, but he eventually drifted off to sleep.

* * * *

His little cabin shook on its foundations in his dream. He felt the ground move under his feet, and he found himself frozen in place as he fought to keep his balance. He needed to run, but shifting his weight even by just a fraction made him nearly topple over, his arms pin wheeling wildly.

Not a sound could come from his throat. Cries of terror as whatever it was outside continued to bang against the walls and the door only managed to squeeze out of him in helpless wheezes.

Boom. Boom. Boom.

What room was he in? Oh. Oh, yes, he was in the garret room, and the horrifying assault on his home had gone up the walls and was now concentrated on the upper half as well as the ceiling, it seemed.

"Stop it!" he shouted, pressing his hands against his ears. "Stop!"

The deafening thuds now moved rapidly along the walls from one end to the other before going up the roof. Darcy looked up and saw the ceiling shake. A terrifying thought since like the rest of the cabin, the roof was just a collection of wooden beams and planks, the outside surface a shell of aging wooden shingles. There wasn't any real insulation anywhere, including the roof.

And as the thing outside continued to bang heavily against it, dust fell onto the floor, some blinding Darcy even has he tried to shield his eyes.

"Stop! Please, stop!"

Sweet child, come out and play! Come, come—it's beautiful out here!

Would you like to watch the moon dance with the stars?

Would you like to see our toys? We have a few you can play with!

Come out!

He'd heard those voices before. He knew that too well. But he couldn't remember when and where—though in dreams? Yes, most likely in dreams. This time the voices wove into each other, tangling and knotting and forming a mess of indecipherable sounds of siren-like calls and encouragement. And Darcy wanted to run in their direction, seek out their comforting arms in the dark. But he shrank back, distancing himself from those voices, though he didn't know why.

"No! I won't!"

Another sound made itself heard amid the din. Something like a male voice, at least to Darcy's confused and overloaded senses.

"Darcy! Darcy, are you there? It's me!"

Torn out of his dream, Darcy sat up with a low, strangled gasp. Remnants of his dream fluttered away in the night in tattered pieces, and awareness of his surroundings gradually took their terrible place.

He was in his room, he found, breathing raggedly and hearing the loud pounding of his heart and the wild rushing of his blood. Barely any light from outside managed to find its way in past the gaps between his small window's curtains. He didn't have a clock anywhere nearby, and his disorientation left him dizzy.

But the voice...

"Darcy! Hey, it's me! Open the door, please! I need to see if you're okay!"

Darcy's gaze flew to the bedroom door and the shadows beyond. The voice was real, he found, and so was the steady but less terrifying pounding on the front door.

"Arlen?"

He kicked the blankets off him and nearly fell off his bed as he scrambled to get out. He felt around for his glasses and put them on once he found them on the nightstand. Then he was stumbling into the living room and turning the lights on. As he'd just suddenly awakened, the burst of familiar dim light felt blinding at first, but it only took him a few seconds to adjust. It was certainly one of those times when he was grateful for such a limited amount of brightness allowed him.

The pounding continued, and Darcy fumbled with the deadbolt and the main lock.

"Arlen?" he stammered, gaping at Arlen's pale and tired features as the man regarded him with clear worry. "What're you doing here at this time?"

"Darcy," Arlen breathed. "You're okay."

"Well—yeah. I was asleep when you—oh, hello."

Something warm and insistent wrapping itself around his leg drew his attention away from Arlen and down to a ridiculously handsome cat that was rubbing itself against him. It was a slim and sleek creature but quite muscular still, its uniquely patterned coat of brownish gold and black making it look like a marbleized feline from ancient legend. Large, intelligent eyes ringed with black stared up at him with clear interest in their amber depths.

"That's my familiar," Arlen said in a quieter voice. He certainly sounded relieved and somewhat more relaxed. "Name's Willie. William. Sometimes I get a massive cute attack and call him Willard or Will-will. He usually just looks totally annoyed when I do."

He glanced down and smiled wryly at his little furry companion.

"Come to think of it, he was born unimpressed with me and the world."

Willie looked up at Arlen and snorted.

"See?"

"Why—oh. Um, come in. You, too, Wills. I can call him Wills, right?"

Willie didn't meow but let out a loud, rumbling purr as he strutted inside, tail high, head up and eyes wide. His beautifully patterned head moved restlessly, turning left and right while he sniffed. Then he ignored his companions and trotted—yes, he trotted—toward the kitchen and then vanished around the corner, where the stairs to the garret were as though he were the king of the land.

Darcy's heart nearly stopped at the sight. If Willie was Arlen's familiar, did it mean he could smell or sense something up there? Some sort of ghostly footprints left by the mothers?

"Wait," he began, but a gentle hand took hold of his arm and held him back. He glanced around and found Arlen pinning him with an earnest look.

"Let him wander around," Arlen said. "It's his job to sniff things out and tell me what he finds."

"But..."

Arlen sighed, his gaze flicking in the direction the cat had taken before returning to Darcy. "Darcy, I kind of know what's happening here. In your cabin, I mean. That's why I'm here, and that's why I'm leaving Willie with you until we sort things out."

Darcy stared at him, eyes widening. "I don't know what you mean," he replied, attempts at indifference or confusion utterly failing as his voice came out in a weak little whimper.

"Something was at your door earlier. I chased it, and it disappeared in the cemetery. For some reason, none of my magic could sense it once I was there. I don't know how long I was in St. Anthony's, using one spell after another to help me read the place, but nothing came of it."

Arlen paused and rubbed his face with both hands, a tired sound hissing out of his throat.

"Can I have some water? I really need to talk to you. I know it's late, and I'm sorry for messing up your sleep, but this can't wait."

Darcy, stunned, nodded and shut the door behind Arlen. He glanced, unsure, in the direction of the stairs but led Arlen to the sofa before numbly moving to the kitchen for a glass of water.

Chapter 12

Arlen was simply bowled over by the shockingly high levels of residual essences that had greeted him when a rumpled and sleepy Darcy opened the door. Even more disturbing was the all-too-clear fact that poor Darcy was utterly unaware of anything. He lived in a tainted environment. He'd absorbed whatever supernatural energies had collected over the years. They'd long become an indelible part of his day-to-day existence.

And now Arlen wondered: how would Darcy respond if he were suddenly taken away from such an environment? It wasn't physical at all, but certainly much worse. All things touched by the otherworld in some way or another were affected on a deeper level. Psychic, mental, emotional—even a combination of all three, instinct and the subconscious, especially, not at all safe from the effects.

Of course, how on earth would Arlen take Darcy away from the only home he'd known? Arlen already knew just how strong Darcy's connection was with the little rustic cabin, even putting up with the barest of modern conveniences.

The previous night, Arlen had seen how limited some of the appliances seemed to function. The stove, in fact, only had one burner working, the refrigerator not keeping food fresh or edible for as long as it should, being so old and barely functioning. Even the lights gave off such weak illumination that it was any wonder Darcy could still read, though Arlen now suspected the poor lights might partly be responsible for Darcy's use of glasses.

The sink had no garbage disposal, and Darcy was obliged to scrape leftover food into the trash. It was a miracle the water heater worked as well as it did.

Arlen drank the water Darcy gave him, and he seated himself on the sofa, patting the empty space beside him for Darcy to take after setting the empty glass down on the coffee table. And Darcy did with a charming little blush Arlen was now growing more and more familiar with—and liking a good deal, at that.

"What's going on, Arlen?" he asked after a moment's awkward pause. "Why'd you bring Willie?"

"Did you hear anything weird earlier? Someone or something knocking on your door?"

Darcy, sleepiness long gone, blinked and stared in drop-jawed surprise at Arlen. "I did," he stammered in a hushed voice. "I was playing my cello upstairs and had to stop when I heard knocking coming from downstairs."

Arlen thought Darcy winced a little when he talked about playing his cello, but he said nothing about it and encouraged him with a quiet word and a nod. He took care to watch Darcy's body language, however, as the way his companion sat—rigid and tense—and the way he wrung his hands on his lap warned Arlen there was something else to all of this.

Did Darcy know far more than he let on? Arlen was too tired at the moment to pursue the question.

Darcy then talked about the way the knocking moved from one part of the cabin to another, the sounds strangely frantic yet soft against the walls till the—creature, whatever it was—reached the front door and proceeded to knock against it with a puzzling desperation that startled even Arlen when he spotted it.

"I think that might've been the moment you got here because I—I swear I heard your voice somewhere outside, but I wasn't too sure. I wondered if I was hallucinating the whole time, but it was kind of impossible for that to be the case." Darcy swallowed, anxiety seemingly doubling as he squirmed even more. "I don't get it. It just came out of nowhere."

Arlen nodded but held his peace in hopes of getting Darcy to talk some more, however meandering his accounts might be. Arlen could easily parse through the jumble despite his exhaustion.

"Why didn't it break the windows? I mean—it kept knocking on the walls and the door, I'm just—kind of shocked that it never went for the windows."

"It kept itself away from the glass. It—it's one of those things that works like a mirror. A mirror's believed to serve as a protection against evil spirits in some cultures, and glass can sometimes offer some protection because of its reflective qualities." Arlen took a deep breath, making sure Darcy met his gaze when he said, "Unless someone in the past had the windows hexed with a minor protection spell. Wouldn't surprise me if that's the case."

It was a subtle—perhaps too subtle—and rather awkwardly spoken hint meant to wring a bit of information from Darcy without freaking out the young man.

"I don't know anything about that," Darcy replied, confusion and worry further darkening his features. His posture stiffened even more, and his hand-wringing never abated. "Why would anyone do that? Like, protection from thieves and stuff? I guess it makes sense, considering where this cabin's built."

Arlen grimaced and shrugged. Apparently that was a failed experiment.

"More on the 'stuff' and less on the 'thieves', I think."

When Darcy's pitiful look of perplexity deepened, Arlen sighed and reached across the space between them to rest a hand on Darcy's restless ones. Happily, that seemed to calm him, and Arlen managed a small smile in relief and encouragement.

"What do you know about your mom or your ancestors?"

"I already told you about my mom. I know nothing about my grandparents and whoever else came before them. Why? Do you think..." Darcy paused, frowning as he mulled things over. "Do you think they practiced some kind of magic?"

"It's a possibility. It sure explains why I spotted that thing knocking on your door. And why I keep sensing this really strong supernatural imprint all over your cabin—and on you."

There. Arlen finally said it, though he felt a bit conflicted before this moment as to whether or not he ought to come out with it then or wait till he had more information to go by. But seeing that horrible apparition earlier had easily thrown him for a loop, and when he'd begun his day quite set in his plans of unraveling the truth, the ghoulish creature convinced him that waiting might not be a good idea, after all.

But what else made him go back and forth about it in his head?

Darcy Winter, he told himself with a sinking spirit.

There was simply no way he was going to keep to a more leisurely schedule of solving a mystery now that he'd spent a decent amount of time with Darcy. Learned more about the lonely young man who might as well live like a hermit in a cave.

How Darcy adored his mother. How he took up the responsibility of keeping his rustic legacy as much in tip-top shape as he could without a word of complaint about the measly conveniences afforded him. How much of a great cook he turned out to be. How selfless and empathic he was toward those unfortunate, nameless souls long forgotten in St. Anthony's.

Darcy had started out as nothing more than a possible subject for observation and even intervention, given the mysterious essences that stubbornly clung to him. He could have been nothing more than a case study.

Now Arlen wasn't so sure, and he blamed himself for letting Darcy in—for allowing Darcy to breach his defenses and his impeccable work ethic. His purpose was now muddled, and while Arlen was usually exceptional when it came to thinking fast on his feet, changing his course in the face of unexpected developments, he now found himself flailing.

Because every time he looked into Darcy's open expressions, doubt after doubt crept in.

Darcy didn't answer him right away. His gaze dropping on Arlen's hand, which continued to rest on his, he sighed and shook his head. "I really don't know. Mom never said anything about magic or sorcerers in my family. I know it sounds kind of hokey, but the only magic she practiced was music. I only inherited a tiny smidge of her talent, and she taught me everything I know."

"Did she tell you your grandparents' names? Or great-grandparents?"

"She might've, but I don't remember." Darcy's wan features creased again as he considered. "The only thing that stands out to me is that every family who lived here was named Winter. So—the fathers, I think? Yeah, I guess the fathers who inherited the name? Oh—also I think every family was pretty tiny, like with one kid. You know, a mom, a dad, and a kid."

"Okay. That's a start."

"What do you mean? Is there something about my family that's somehow connected to what happened tonight?"

Arlen pulled his hand away and rubbed it against his face. He felt so tired now, and if he could, he'd simply crash where he sat. The toll from that evening's hunt as well as the unplanned chase was greater than he expected, and the initial rush of adrenaline had dissipated and left him with a pretty rotten feeling.

"It's possible. I mean, it's the only plausible reason I can come up with that might explain everything weird that's happened here. And the fact that your family's been holding on to the cabin for so long. Your grandparents' lawyers and a PI even had to hunt your mom down, so she could come back and take her place here."

He was about to say something else when his link to his familiar tingled, and he heard Willie's voice in his head.

Touched by the dead. Many were here. They stayed but didn't harm. Darcy safe.

Really, now? Arlen couldn't help but blink in some amazement at what he'd just learned.

Protection and companionship. Darcy very good with companionship.

"Yes, he is, isn't he?"

"What was that?"

"Huh?" Arlen blinked again. Then he realized he'd just absentmindedly replied to his familiar's psychic communication with a verbal one. "Oh—nothing. I was just thinking out loud."

Darcy, bless him, didn't appear convinced, but he said nothing. At that moment Willie made his appearance, emerging from the kitchen area and trotting over to them.

"Meeowr. Owrr."

Darcy started and glanced back. "Jesus, he's got lungs. Does he meow that loud, usually?"

"Only when he wants attention." Arlen smiled at the sight of Willie meeting Darcy's wide-eyed gaze without hesitation and then walking over to him and jumping onto his lap. "He definitely wants yours now."

The purring that followed was loud as Darcy stroked the cat's sleek fur, his features lighting up and imbuing his face with a beauty that again left Arlen breathless. Willie nudged and rubbed, marking Darcy with his scent even as he continued his communication with Arlen.

Protect Darcy. Always protect Darcy for Arlen.

What did you find upstairs, buddy?

Ghosts. Dead long, long ago. Sad ghosts. Lost and confused. Need Darcy. Can't let Darcy go.

I don't understand. What do you mean by that?

Need Darcy. Their son. Need their son. Need something they were denied. Won't let go. Can't let go.

Wait, what? Did you say their son? He's their son?

They think it. They wish. They love.

Arlen pinched his mouth and watched Darcy lose himself momentarily in Willie, lavishing the cat with attention and adoration while murmuring nonsensical baby talk and occasionally chuckling.

Well, he thought, *there* was the complication he feared. If those ghosts—whoever they were once upon a time—had formed a strong and unbreakable connection with Darcy, the idea of forcibly severing that connection for Darcy's sake was going to be a much, much bigger risk than he'd first believed. Vengeful ghosts were a terrifying force to be reckoned with.

Chapter 13

Darcy had to cancel his interview and call in sick at work. He simply couldn't function after the dreadful excitement—if one were to call it that—from the previous night. Benjamin was, naturally, understanding and even convinced him to take a couple of paid days off.

"Dude, you've earned it. You've been working here for two years now, and you haven't even asked for a week off. Have you been checking your pay stubs? Did you see how many paid days off you've collected?"

Benjamin said, laughing. Darcy could imagine his boss and good friend shaking his head at the other end of the line as they spoke.

"Take it easy and rest up, buddy. We're good here. I'm just making sure Zoe gets her coffee, and it'll be non-stop energy till closing. She'll be doing the job of five people."

Darcy chuckled. "Okay, cool. Thanks, Benjamin. Um—I'll go feed the cat and then go back to bed."

"Cat? You got yourself a cat? When did this happen?"

"Last night, I guess. Or early this morning. Uh—the cat's Arlen's familiar."

Benjamin didn't say a word for a handful of seconds. "Seriously, man? A magical cat? That's pretty sick! Wait—why would Arlen leave his familiar with you? Don't sorcerers need their familiars to draw some of their powers from or something weird-ass like that?"

"It's kind of a long story, and I'll tell you as soon as I'm back at work."

Movement just off to the side drew Darcy's attention from the living room picture window to the dining area, and he smiled at the sight of Willie basking in the morning sun.

The cat sat where there sunlight spilled onto the floor, between the dining table and the sideboard, his face turned up and his eyes closed in a show of utter contentment and relaxation. Darcy wondered if familiars also drew some of their powers from sunlight or moonlight (perhaps both?), and he marveled at the way the cat's sleek coat shimmered.

"Okay, dude. But don't rush back, okay? We'd rather have you miss out on a few days than see you show up a total wreck. You deserve the break." Benjamin made a thoughtful little sound before proceeding. "Tell you what. Take three days off, paid. I want you healthy and clear-headed when you come back. All right?"

"But..."

"I'm your boss. You listen to me."

Darcy laughed. "Yes, sir."

"Awesome. We'll see you in three days, then."

The call ended with Darcy staring at his phone—the only technologically advanced convenience he owned—in mute shock.

No, he never once called in sick since Benjamin hired him, now that his attention was drawn to the fact. He'd definitely amassed an insane number of paid days off, and he had to make use of them and ensure he didn't get into any trouble with any state labor laws pertaining to those if any existed.

He sighed and put his phone down on the coffee table, glancing around and feeling himself suddenly at a loss as to how best to spend his day.

Oh, yes, feed the cat first.

Arlen had stopped by just an hour ago on his way to the Arcane Institute to drop off Willie's food and food bowls as well as the litter box and sand. He'd also checked to make sure the cat's collar—a hexed one that provided excellent protection to the familiar and to its current keeper (Darcy in this case)—was properly on.

"Make sure to let him out for a couple of hours. He needs to wander around and read the area for me. He might even go to the cemetery if something draws his attention to it. Don't worry if he does or if he doesn't answer to your call later. He'll come back to you when he's good and ready."

Darcy glanced at the distant road and watched a rusty old VW van chug past.

"How about the road? Aren't you worried he'd get hit?"

"Familiars never get hurt. Seriously, they don't. If a familiar was in any danger of getting run over, there's a way higher chance of the vehicle being forced aside and probably running off the road," Arlen replied, dropping to one knee to give Willie one last chin rub and a kiss. "Keep an eye on Darcy, okay, buddy? He's very special."

Darcy could have sworn his face just burst into flames at that, but he just watched the pair bond for a few seconds before Arlen had to go. He wasn't sure, but in that final moment of silence, there was an intensity in the way sorcerer and familiar looked at each other even with the gentle chin rubs. It was as though they spoke with each other telepathically.

This was magic, however, and Darcy wouldn't know up from down when it came to it. As long as he had clear instructions on how best to care for his temporary pet and guardian, he was content.

"Okay, Wills," he said as he marched past the cat and headed for the kitchen. "Breakfast time."

"Mreowr. Owrr. Owrr! *Owwwr! Owwwwwrr!*" With every meow, Willie's voice intensified by a decibel.

"God, you're loud. That's a pretty powerful pair of lungs you've got there."

"Owrr! Owrr!" Willie apparently loved listening to himself howl at full volume. *"Yowrr! Yowrr!"*

Darcy rolled his eyes and laughed as he opened a small can of wet food and scooped the contents out and into one of the bowls. He found a spot for Willie's meals next to the sideboard, and soon he was leaning against the counter, sipping his breakfast tea, while watching the cat clean one bowl and then move on to drink water from the other.

Darcy found the idle moment pleasing and wonderfully domestic, his thoughts straying over to dangerous territory when he started to picture Arlen finishing the quiet little scene.

Perhaps Arlen would be sitting at the table, eating his breakfast and chatting about strange experiences with an easy and indifferent air about him. Hauntings, hunts, magic in all forms, the history of magic or other things well outside Darcy's purview—those subjects would be mundane to Arlen and easy subjects to discuss over breakfast.

He imagined the conversation to somewhere along the lines of "How was work, honey? Oh, another creepster from the world of the dead? How'd you handle that one?"

But it was nothing more than fanciful thinking, Darcy told himself.

Arlen's questions about his history, particularly his family, had left a bit of a sour taste in Darcy's mouth, and he couldn't forget or shake it off so easily. It touched on a question he'd asked himself several times over since Arlen asked him out on a date. Arlen's interest made him feel good and hopeful then, but in the harsh light of day—and after a bit of time between then and now—Darcy's hopes were proving to be more chimera than real.

No, he corrected himself. The doubt that had been clawing away at him didn't touch on a question. It answered it. A dull ache now throbbed in his chest, forcing Darcy to rub it in a vain effort at soothing the pain.

Arlen wasn't interested in Darcy *like that.* He'd asked him out on a date to know more about his past because of whatever dark mojo had somehow attached itself to him and left him reeking of supernatural stuff that only sorcerers could sniff. Darcy had been marked by magic, and Arlen needed to know more.

His gaze dropped to his empty cup, his eyes misting.

"I knew it was too good to be true," he muttered, shaking his head in disgust at himself for even daring to entertain the stupid possibility that anyone like Arlen Stroescu would be interested in him for, well, normal reasons. He blinked rapidly till the tears receded. "Dumb. Dumb, dumb, dumb."

He turned and set his cup into the sink, any need for breakfast now gone.

He's very special.

Arlen's final words to Willie had everything to do with the whole mojo-touched thing. Funny how ghosts made one special, he thought. That would be it and nothing more.

He glanced behind him and eyed the stairs leading to the loft. The mothers had to be the reason for his being mojo-touched. They'd been to the cabin since his childhood, had been soothed with music by his mother and now him. *Of course* they'd leave residual imprints or whatever sorcerers called them on everything they'd come in contact with. Even if they never touched Darcy, they'd still...

Darcy's eyes widened as something vague suddenly flashed in his mind.

A memory. Something that had happened a long, long time ago. Something that had happened to him, in fact, he now realized as he struggled to catch that elusive, gossamer strand of memory. It vanished just as quickly as it appeared, though, but it left a strong enough impression to keep Darcy wondering.

"The mothers?" he whispered, frowning. He looked back again at the stairs. "What about the mothers?"

Touch, a distant voice from some unknown depths reminded him. Touch.

The mothers had touched him? Had somehow come in physical contact with him sometime ago? Why couldn't he remember?

It was likely a memory he'd inadvertently jogged by thinking about the mothers and their midnight visits. Some sort of connection was made, a triggering event that somehow led him down that curious path. Try as he might, however, nothing else came up, and before long he gave up the fight.

With a heavy sigh, he tugged the short curtains open and stared out the kitchen window. The scene outside was quite pretty, the morning softened by a little bit of mist. The sun still poured over the area, and Darcy could hear the cheerful twittering of birds outside.

Well, he might as well make something of his day off. He didn't have TV and used his phone for entertainment, largely, though he still preferred books to streaming films and shows. But the option of passively watching something didn't sound attractive then, and he found himself back on square one, wondering and a touch annoyed.

He again thought of the mothers and how they skittered away last night, terrified of the creature that had suddenly forced itself into their quiet world. Pity again overtook him, and Darcy finally settled on a plan.

He thought about Arlen's accounts, and in the light of the morning sun, Darcy found the idea less nerve-wracking. He should go back to the cemetery and keep up with the trimming and all that. He had plenty of time now, and perhaps he might be able to find some sort of clue about Arlen's Monster (as he now called it) in the unforgiving light of day.

Besides, he told himself, looking down at Willie, who now sat by his feet, hard at work licking his paws and cleaning himself off, he now had a companion. Darcy had to smile ruefully. No, Arlen might not be into him at all, but he was sweet and considerate and was determined to keep him safe, even sending his own familiar there to keep an eye on Darcy.

Darcy knelt on the floor to stroke Willie's fur and give him a quick kiss.

"Whoever it is your dad falls in love with will be a really lucky guy," he whispered, his smile faltering, and he swallowed thickly. "And when that happens, you'll have your paws full looking after him as well."

Willie met his tear-fogged gaze with eyes as large and as bright as ever, and for some reason, Darcy thought he heard the cat snort derisively. No, it was just his imagination, he told himself, but there still seemed to be a decidedly unimpressed air rolling out of the cat in thick waves. If Willie had eyebrows, one would be cocked high.

Chapter 14

If the library's guardian were corporeal and had a complete body, it would be regarding Arlen with its hands on its hips, one foot tapping a mad rhythm on the floor, and one eye twitching.

But the Arcane Institute's own was, naturally, nothing more than a pair of spectral hands that gesticulated and communicated strictly with pointed fingers or an emphatic (or dismissive) wave. Now and then, when impatience got the better of it, the guardian would spell a rather terse message on the nearest wall with a finger, its words getting carved into the paint and plaster, where they'd remain for no more than fifteen or so seconds before fading completely.

Arlen himself had been on the receiving end of a random Latin phrase he eventually discovered to be a pretty colorful way of saying "stop being such a motherfucking idiot" on the wall when he'd bothered the guardian with a touch too much vehemence because he was just in a foul mood that day. That morning, he tried his damnedest not to be too much of a pain in the invisible rear for the guardian.

"There's got to be something about St. Anthony's cemetery," he said, refusing to budge from the counter.

The guardian merely drummed the fingers of both hands on the polished wood.

"It's reeking with all kinds of otherworld energies and imprints. I've already told you about the thing I saw that disappeared into the cemetery when I went after it."

The drumming stopped, and the guardian immediately scribbled on the counter. It was a testament to its remarkable abilities that it managed to spell out a complete message upside-down because Arlen could easily read it from his side of the counter.

I thought you said before there was nothing to be read over there.

"Well, that's the point, though, right? Why would it be a dead place on every level but suddenly be haunted by that—pretty disturbing specimen of a ghost?"

Arlen couldn't help a grimace and an involuntary shudder at the remembrance. He'd seen just about everything that could be seen during his hunts, but nothing had prepared him for the stratospheric levels of wrongness in the specter he'd encountered.

Perhaps it was because it was clearly haunting an unsuspecting Darcy that added to Arlen's revulsion—and anxiety. At least Willie was there, keeping an eye on Darcy while closely observing the cemetery, the cabin, and their immediate environment. The protection spell Arlen had also surreptitiously cast on the cabin should help his familiar.

Again, however, the moment he'd reached the cemetery, all sense of life immediately vanished in the darkness. In the light of day, the feeling was quite unnerving, but in the dead of night, it was simply horrifying.

It felt like tumbling into a void. A vacuum. There were the usual night sounds of crickets and the quiet restlessness of the evening breeze, but they all seemed to function on a wholly separate plane, their existence seemingly limited to everywhere else but St. Anthony's.

Arlen had taken great care to cast several phantom fires all over the cemetery in a bid to chase away as many shadows as he possibly could, but even those magical fiery balls of light failed to reveal anything.

Like gigantic fireflies, they moved about in the air some five feet above ground, lighting up the desolate burial ground from end to end while Arlen moved quickly around, searching desperately for his quarry. He'd even sent three phantom fires into the wood beyond, and he watched them dance and weave their cheerful way through the trees, but as before, none of them helped.

Several minutes later, Arlen was obliged to give up the search and summon the lights back, the swirling balls of fire moving into each other till only one was left, and it guided an exhausted Arlen back to the cabin.

The phantom had specifically directed him to the cemetery. It wanted him to go there, though for what reason, he didn't know. And being baited and then left hanging like that got on his last nerve.

Have you considered maybe a curse of some kind?

"Curse? On the cemetery?"

The drumming commenced, which was the guardian's way of communicating something rather snarky like "Gee, you think?"

"Maybe? I do think the Winter family's got something to do with that cemetery. From what Darcy told me, his great-great-grandparents lived in that cabin, and everyone else after that pretty much inherited the place. Darcy's grandparents broke the chain, in a way, by moving out. His mom never lived in that place till after she got pregnant with Darcy, and even she had to be hunted down by the family lawyer and a PI they hired."

It's possible the Winter family was cursed if a curse is involved in this case.

And that was why nobody could leave, Arlen thought, frowning. Every descendant—or every generation down the line *had* to live in the cabin. If the supernatural connection between the cabin, the family, and the cemetery was, indeed, real, it was no wonder poor Darcy was swaddled in those essences. And it was no wonder the cabin's interior nearly stopped Arlen in his tracks with the alarmingly overpowering levels of otherworld energies and imprints bearing down on him from all sides.

With Darcy's grandparents breaking the line of owners, however, Arlen wondered what had happened during those years of silence. How did the unoccupied cabin fare? Pretty well, apparently, given its perfectly preserved state. And the cemetery and its silent residents? Arlen couldn't begin to guess.

"What would the connection with the cemetery be, though? And that weird ghost I chased?"

The guardian didn't answer right away, the drumming taking on a slightly different tone—if such a word could be used. It had turned rather thoughtful.

Who's buried in St. Anthony's?

"I don't know. Even Darcy, who's sweet and thoughtful enough to take the time to clean up the place whenever he can, doesn't know. Gloria and I've been there. None of the gravestones have names on them. I mean, they've all been pretty much wiped out by the weather over the years. Even the vault in the middle of the cemetery doesn't have any sort of ID on it and is pretty much falling to pieces. The whole cemetery itself is in a really sad state."

Arlen went on and continued to describe the cemetery in greater detail at the urging of the guardian. When he finally ran out of things to add, a momentary pause fell. Even the guardian's drumming ceased, and for a second or two, Arlen wondered if a pair of spectral hands was capable of falling asleep.

Let's look at the deaths recorded around the middle of the 19th century.

Arlen perked up. "The library's got records?"

Naturally. It's the Arcane Institute, buster. We own all the weird shit through history.

No wonder the regular public library gave him little to nothing to go by. Arlen wished he'd gone to the Arcane Institute library's prickly guardian first. That certainly would have saved him some time.

"Lead on, then," Arlen said, grinning, and bowed with a grandiose flourish.

Smartass. Let's go.

The next half hour was spent scouring through the less-visited and more shadowy corners of the library on the third floor, situated well toward the back of the building.

The records section, which was housed there, even looked like a crypt but well-lit, at least as long as the sun was up. The arched ceiling and narrow hallway of shelves ended with a wall and a matching arched window that allowed sunlight through.

Dust motes floated everywhere, and in the slanted beams, the guardian's ghostly shape could be made out slightly. A hunched and twisted figure of a man in classic Victorian costume flickered in and out of view. And even when it did, Arlen saw it was more like a vague silhouette than anything more definite. The hands, however, remained clearer and more substantial, though still quite translucent.

He'd seen the library's guardian's figure before, always whenever the sunlight struck it, but not once had its face revealed itself. Even when the guardian paused, completely awash in sunlight, its face remained dark and indistinguishable.

It was as though it were cursed to stay in the shadows and kept from being identified by anyone. Students and staff were quite used to its otherworldly peculiarities, and Arlen never batted an eye.

The guardian paused before a shelf, its hands busily skimming over ancient spines. Then it pulled a thin and narrow volume out, showing the date to Arlen with an emphatic and triumphant jab of a finger (1865) before opening the book and beckoning Arlen over as it moved closer to the window.

The two of them huddled together in silence as they read through the listing.

Yes, it was a record of deaths in Dolores in 1865, the faded and partly smudged ink barely readable in places but still offering Arlen a treasure trove of information.

The guardian paused its page-flipping somewhere past the middle of the book and tapped the pages excitedly. Arlen read through the list, his breath catching.

It was a list of deceased women, all of whom apparently had died in childbirth. None of them had been married, and surprisingly enough, they were buried in St. Anthony's. Only twelve were listed as those unfortunate mothers who'd been laid to rest in that cemetery, while whoever else came after were buried elsewhere.

And, tragically, all of them were quite young. Three were in their mid-teens.

It appeared as though St. Anthony's was taking in the dead for a brief period of time before all burial services stopped for some reason. Of course, a host of ordinary and quite logical reasons could be behind its sudden cessation, but something told Arlen there must have been something more to it than that. The land surrounding St. Anthony's was quite spacious, and he could imagine back in the day when the road cutting through the rural fringes of the city wasn't around meant so much more ground for burial purposes.

"I wonder who's interred in the vault, then," he murmured, frowning at the names.

The guardian immediately flipped pages till it reached the last dozen or so. After another brief moment of skimming over fading cursive writing, it drew Arlen's attention to a passage near the bottom of one page. It appeared to be a section of the city's records that provided some information about certain places of interest—in this case, cemeteries.

St. Anthony's, it appeared, had been owned by a Gregory Winter, a millionaire who'd also been a devout Catholic in his lifetime. He'd established St. Anthony's as a means of honoring unwed mothers who died in childbirth. The cemetery had shut down, however, with no reason given, and Winter was laid to rest in the vault among the young mothers he'd tried to honor in death.

Like a protective and loving father looking after his children. A guardian even in death.

Arlen scrunched up his face as he read and reread the passage. It certainly made a good deal of sense, providing him with some context behind the nature of the cemetery, but there was also too much that had been hidden away and kept from public records. That much was pretty obvious to him. If anything, the more he learned about St. Anthony's history, the muddier the waters seemed to get, and he felt he knew even less than ever.

Chapter 15

Darcy straightened with a groan, grimacing as he stretched his limbs and his back. He'd completely lost track of time, and it had been a pretty productive morning on the whole. With no other obligations to deal with, he'd managed to spend as much time as he could taking care of St. Anthony's, and before he knew it, a good three hours had passed. He'd never even stopped for a quick break.

The mist had long gone, and nothing but the brilliant, late summer sun bathed the area. Birds flew here and there, rending the silence with their songs and light calls, while now and then, the distant sound of a car or two driving past drew his attention from his work.

Darcy gazed around him and grinned despite his exhaustion. He'd cleared up a good deal of overgrowth, the lawn bags sitting just outside the cemetery gates packed to nearly bursting. Perhaps it was a good thing in the end that he didn't bother to bring extra bags, as he would have continued to clean up St. Anthony's till the sun set.

"Yowrrr! Meowwr!"

He laughed softly at the shrill howls of his furry escort. Chaperone, really. Somewhere in the cemetery Willie had wandered, picking his way through weeds and vines with an ease, confidence, and speed that left Darcy impressed beyond words. Now and then the cat would call out to him as though ensuring he knew he wasn't left alone.

"I'm ready to go home, Wills," he called back.

Darcy spent the next few minutes packing up his tools and moving them out, so that they all sat together with the filled lawn bags. He went back inside the cemetery to look for Willie and see if everything was all right with the cat. He didn't need to force him back home, as per Arlen's instructions, but he still didn't feel that comfortable leaving the cat alone in the cemetery, magic or no magic.

"Wills? Where are you?"

A harsh breath being blown out suddenly broke the silence, and Darcy stumbled to a halt.

"What..."

He turned around, searching the gravestones for a sign of another person, but he was alone. The sound of someone letting out a loud, raspy breath again came, this time drawing his attention elsewhere as he tried to map its source. A couple more times of the same eerie, disembodied exhalation, and Darcy found himself staring nervously at the crumbling old vault.

From somewhere nearby, Willie started growling. A low, sustained warning that only exacerbated Darcy's unease.

"Wills? Wills! Over here!"

Willie didn't respond, however, and continued to growl. When movement just off to the side drew Darcy's attention briefly away from the vault, he spotted Willie creeping through the tall grass and weeds, his attention fixed on the vault, it seemed. The cat was in full hunting mode, at least from what little Darcy knew about feline behavior. Slowly and steadily, Willie inched forward, keeping his body low, his eyes fixed on the vault ahead.

Darcy couldn't just leave. Despite the clear signs of an unseen threat, he simply refused to leave Arlen's familiar there, alone to face whatever Willie sensed as a danger.

"Damn it," Darcy muttered as he inched his way forward as well, taking good care to keep the cat within sight.

One false move, and he'd startle the cat. And the last thing he needed was a missing familiar or a face, arms, and hands covered in scratches and blood.

He watched Willie creep closer to the vault, stopping momentarily at the top of the stone steps leading down to the vault's sealed entrance. The cat stayed there, his body still kept low and unmoving as he continued to watch the vault and growl.

Another sound came—another ragged exhalation that Darcy now knew came from the vault. From within its crumbling and discolored brick and mortar, as if the structure itself had just exhaled. Even more troubling was the idea of someone inside the vault—alive or perhaps undead, seeking a way out. Willie growled again and then followed that with a loud hiss, though he never moved an inch.

At that point, Darcy had had enough. Throwing caution to the wind, he hurried forward and scooped up the cat before fleeing the cemetery with Willie, who appeared not to even notice what was happening to him and continued to growl and hiss while looking over Darcy's shoulder the whole time.

He felt stiff and still ready to pounce as Darcy held him. Apparently the cat refused to take his eyes off the vault, clearly for good reason, but Darcy wasn't about to hang around and find out why.

"Okay, buddy, that's enough," Darcy stammered, panting as he squeezed through the crooked gates. "Let's go home. You're staying put in the cabin with me, okay? And I don't give a shit what your boss says about that."

Cradling Willie against his chest with one hand, he carried the bucket filled with his tools with the other and loped back to the cabin. The three filled lawn bags would have to wait. Perhaps later, Arlen would stop by and help him bring those back to the cabin. The brief incident was simply too frightening for Darcy to brave three return trips to St. Anthony's—even with the sun still high above. There was no way he was going back there without a warm-blooded human companion at his side.

Preferably one who was pretty handy at using magic.

* * * *

Arlen's familiar remained on edge for a good while after their return. While Darcy cleaned around the cabin, he kept an eye on Willie, who refused to sit still.

Letting out impatient huffs and even occasional chirps that reeked of muttered complaints, the cat would trot from room to room, pausing before a picture window and standing on his hind legs in order to peer out for a handful of seconds. Then he'd turn and go past the kitchen and up the stairs to the loft, all this time behaving as though Darcy didn't exist.

From where Darcy stood at the kitchen counter, he'd listen to Willie huff and chirp impatiently upstairs as well before going back down the stairs and repeating his movements.

Darcy felt as though he were watching a caged wild animal just itching to break free. That said, he also noticed that Willie wasn't fighting to get out. He never once went to either the front door or the side door and paw away at the wood, crying or letting out whatever temperamental feline sounds he had in his vocal arsenal.

No, Willie seemed to be restlessly guarding the cabin, ensuring nothing threatening was hovering nearby—at least in Darcy's eyes.

"Settle down, buddy," he said in as quiet and gentle a voice as he could when Willie passed him for the fifth or sixth time. "Settle down. Want me to call your dad?"

Not that Willie was expected to answer either way, really, and Darcy realized how ridiculous he must have looked just then. With a sigh, he turned around and finished putting together his usual sandwich. As he set the soiled utensils in the sink, he glanced up and looked through the kitchen window and nearly dropped the empty glass he held.

The cemetery's entrance could be glimpsed from there, and he spotted the lawn bags resting against the rusty fence.

The gates, however, were open.

Wide open, at that.

From where he stood, Darcy could see the two wrought iron barriers barely hanging on to their ancient and rusty hinges. One of the gates moved in the breeze, its crooked and sadly misshapen pickets shifting as the entire thing swung ever so slightly. At least it seemed so from where Darcy stood, gaping in stunned silence at the sight.

Darcy had taken care to keep the gates secured even when he was fleeing the cemetery. It was pretty easy to manage given the way the gates had always been stuck in one position for as long as Darcy remembered. Their hinges had always felt as though they'd been fused solid over time, keeping the gates fixed in that one partly open position for years. Darcy himself had tried to move them several times, but they refused to budge, their bottom halves also secured against movement by a tangle of thick vines.

That morning, he'd even regretted filling the lawn bags he brought with him because it had proven to be a massive pain to force them through the gates. Once or twice, Darcy wondered if any of the bags he carried was in any danger of being ripped open by the misshapen iron and its broken and jutting ornamentation.

There was simply no way for the gates to move, let alone be forced wide open by the breeze.

The gates also made a good deal of noise when being forced apart during entry or exit. Surely Darcy would have heard them as they swung apart, even from a distance. The general area was so peaceful that sound carried easily. It was damn near impossible for Darcy not to hear anything amiss from the safety of his home.

Darcy swallowed, the earlier unease now returning despite the safety of his cabin and the presence of a familiar.

He left his sandwich on the counter and ran to the living room, swiping his phone off the coffee table and immediately calling Arlen. Of course, Arlen didn't answer, as he was very likely in the middle of a lecture or a tutoring session, but Darcy refused to hang up. He hurried back to the kitchen and peered out, keeping his gaze on the distant gates.

"Hi, Arlen?" he stammered. "It's Darcy. Listen—something's going on over at St. Anthony's. If you could call me back as soon as you get this message, that'll be great. Um—don't worry about Willie. I have him here, all safe and sound but definitely weirded out by something he sensed in the cemetery. Oh, yeah, that's—that's another thing I want to talk to you about. Just—please call me back, okay? It's really important."

Darcy swallowed, suddenly at a loss for words after blurting things out in a fearful jumble that barely made sense in his own head. When he disconnected the call, he went around the cabin to check all windows and doors, even sprinting upstairs to ensure the garret was safely secured and then downstairs to the bathroom.

Every time, he looked out and nervously scanned the area and only feeling faint relief from seeing nothing but sunlit grass, trees, and the distant road.

When he took his place at the table, his sandwich and his glass of water awaiting his pleasure, he spotted Willie sitting on the sofa, looking rather stiff and on full alert as he stared, unblinking, at the nearest picture window. The cat appeared to be searching the outside for something—or perhaps waiting for something to appear. Willie's tenseness was certainly catching.

Darcy ate his lunch in unhappy silence, occasionally glancing at the dining room's window in mimicry of Willie's vigilance. Unlike Arlen's familiar, however, Darcy didn't feel at all ready for a fight, and the fact that something terrifying was up and about in full daylight only served to heighten his nervousness, turning his stomach into knots and threatening a full-on regurgitation of his modest lunch.

And there was certainly no way he was in the right frame of mind to turn to his cello for comfort.

"Looks like I'll be binge-watching something on my phone, after all," he muttered, casting another anxious look at the dining room's picture window.

The primeval beauty of the landscape outside now seemed hollow and insidious in a creeping, stealthy way, even in the clear light of the midday sun.

Chapter 16

Time's up. The library will be closing in five minutes.

"What, already?"

Yes, already. Come back for those tomorrow. We can place them on reserve for you.

Reluctantly Arlen shut the ancient book, nearly sneezing from the familiar whiff of old paper laced with dust and dried up bookbinding glue. He saw just how many volumes he'd managed to snatch from shelves barely frequented by staff and students alike, and he was mightily glad such an obscure subject had been his focus.

Of course, obscurity also meant nothing more than snippets of information being gleaned from pages of historical facts and accounts. The proverbial needle in a haystack. At least he'd also taken great care to copy by hand whatever information he found, and a pleasurable wave swept over him at the sight of so many sheets of paper he'd filled up.

"I really appreciate that," he said at length as he gathered the books into one neat pile. "Thanks so much for your help."

It's no problem at all.

Before long Arlen was walking briskly down the empty hallway toward the exit, glancing at his watch and grimacing at the time. He wondered if Willie had found anything while out and about earlier that day, seeing as how he never received messages from his familiar throughout his frenzied research and note-taking. But no problem, he decided, when his thoughts strayed to Darcy, which coaxed a ghost of a smile to curl his mouth. Arlen could always go out and get something to go and bring it with him to Darcy's cabin.

"Hey you," Efrain's voice cut through the happy fog in Arlen's head.

Arlen didn't stop, but he slowed down to allow his friend to reach him. Efrain grinned and slapped him on the shoulder once they fell into step.

"How's the stalking coming along?"

"Oh, ha-ha. You're so funny."

It took a moment for Efrain to calm down from a bout of obnoxious sniggering. "I know. Leander says the same thing before kicking me out of the bedroom after I try to crack a bad joke. So how're things going with Darcy?"

Arlen didn't need any more prodding. Taking a deep breath, he immediately plunged into as detailed and as vivid an account as he could manage about his ghostly chase and the ongoing mystery of St. Anthony's deadness.

From there, he proceeded to share some of the information he'd gathered from that day's research. Efrain listened in respectful silence, his head bowed as he took everything in, even allowing Arlen a few seconds' peace before speaking.

It felt good talking to someone about his dilemma. At least he had his peers at the Arcane Institute to turn to for advice and help, which, of course, naturally led him down more dour paths as he extended those thoughts to poor Darcy and his solitary life. Even if Darcy were to open up to Benjamin about what might be troubling him on a supernatural level, Benjamin wasn't a sorcerer and wouldn't know the first thing about unreadable imprints and otherworldly energies.

"Sounds almost like a family curse, doesn't it?" Efrain noted, his voice a thoughtful hum. "The way I'm seeing this, this Gregory Winter tried to do something good for women everyone rejected back in the day, but something happened that made the cemetery shut down. Winter was then buried with his—mothers—maybe as a symbolic show of support? Since he was apparently the only one to show compassion to those women, it was probably only right he was laid to rest with them. Sort of like a guardian in death."

"I thought that, too. But how does that turn into a family curse?"

"Not really sure, but something tells me Darcy's mom, grandparents, great-grandparents, etc., were all pretty much stuck in that cabin, most likely because that was where Gregory Winter lived, and they continued to help the souls of those mothers in some way or another."

Bound to the cabin—in very much the same way ghosts tended to be bound to places where either they'd died or had spent a good deal of time when alive. The Winter family, in a sense, were like corporeal ghosts, haunting the little cabin for some purpose directly linked to the cemetery and its forgotten sleepers.

"How would they be doing it, though? And why the hell would they be punished with something pretty bizarre like this?" Arlen demanded.

They'd reached the half-empty parking lot by now, and Efrain escorted him to his car. Arlen leaned against the hood on the driver's side, cradling his binder of notes against his chest as he glared at a vague point in the distance.

"I don't even know why Gregory Winter owned such a dinky little cabin when he was a freaking millionaire back then."

"Well, he was religious and stuff. Maybe he was one of the good ones, know what I mean? He didn't care much for his money and used his time and resources to help people who weren't so lucky. And as for himself, I'm guessing he just stuck with the basics and nothing more. You know, just enough of day-to-day necessities to live on."

"I guess that makes sense. It's just too bad nothing else was written about what happened to the cemetery and why it shut down. Then again…" Arlen considered, pursing his lips as his gaze strayed to the dimming sky above. "If he was devout, maybe there was some kind of resistance to his work. Maybe some people didn't like seeing a good man waste his energy on women others would've considered to be hopeless sinners and shit."

"I wouldn't put it past them—past all those old-timey Christian hypocrites. Chances are good they forced the cemetery to shut down."

Arlen snorted. "Old-timey hypocrites—yeah, they're still around. Unfortunately."

And with any luck, Gregory Winter had stood defiant to the end, demanding in his last will that he be buried in a vault among those poor creatures he'd tried to honor with a decent place for their final rest.

Arlen didn't want to entertain possibilities of the man somehow being instrumental—actively instrumental—in the cemetery's shutting down, given what he'd done so selflessly. All of what they were now seeing would have to be because of something else that had been completely beyond Winter's control.

As for the man's descendants and their strange role in all of this? Arlen needed to sit Darcy down and hammer him with even more questions. The apparition he'd chased continued to leave distressing marks in Arlen's mind, mysterious, airy fingerprints that faded quickly but left lingering feelings of doubt and unease, that element of danger hovering just beyond reach.

Bit by bit, Arlen was growing more convinced that Darcy was both the cause of the emerging danger as well as the innocent victim of it.

"By the way, I've got to talk to you about something—kind of important—sometime soon," Efrain piped up just as he made a move toward his own car. He glanced back over his shoulder and flashed Arlen a somewhat nervous smile.

"Yeah, sure. Any hints?"

"Uh—something about proposing to Leander."

Arlen didn't have anything to say to that. He merely stood there, his car keys hanging rather limply from his lifeless hand, and gaped at his retreating friend as Efrain turned around and jogged toward his car. Arlen finally got his brain to reset the moment Efrain got inside and started the engine.

"Wait, what?"

"I'm planning to propose to Leander!" Efrain yelled from his car after rolling the window down. He flashed a huge, blinding grin. "Might as well make an honest man out of him, right?"

"What the—seriously? You're getting hitched?"

Efrain merely rolled his eyes and let out an exaggerated sigh, and the immensity of what Arlen had just heard from his good friend and colleague finally, *finally* sank in.

"I'm buying lunch if that's the case!" he called, and Efrain grinned again, waved, and gave a thumbs up before driving off.

"Well, I'll be damned. Badass Efrain Thorley getting married," Arlen breathed as he watched the car vanish past the low stone walls and merge onto the quiet side street that would take Efrain into the main thoroughfare. "Wow. Kind of feel sorry for Leander."

He got inside his car after shaking his head in amazement, but he simply sat behind the wheel, his own mind whirling at the notion of commitments and devoted, loving relationships.

He'd borne witness to a few, though he'd always been the spectator from start to finish, offering support, a shoulder to cry on, and an occasional kick up the backside whenever irrational fears reared their unwanted heads. As far as he knew, every relationship he'd watched from the initial bloom to the final connection of marriage had been quite happy.

Granted, there were still two or three older couples he hadn't seen in a while, so he couldn't really say for sure how their marriages were coming along.

At least Efrain Thorley's two-year-old relationship with Leander Caron had been one for the romance books. Arlen found himself a tad mystified over the strange workings of Fortune. How in the world did one know, anyway, that the person standing before them was *the one?*

Some people spent an entire lifetime reaching that point. Others made such a discovery so early on in their lives—like Efrain and Leander. The rest of the world simply fell somewhere on that spectrum.

Arlen himself wasn't quite sure where his own life fit in the grand scheme of things. Sorcerer work had been his entire universe, in a way, and despite any growing fondness he felt toward Darcy Winter, Arlen couldn't imagine his world shifting so drastically anytime soon.

"Maybe when I reach thirty or something," he muttered, a crooked little smile forming. "I should be in total control of my life by then."

Then he winced when he heard his irate parents' voices shrieking about the cruelty of Fate and why no decent fellow out there was willing to take their son off their hands. In fact, his mother had recently threatened to play matchmaker, which only added to Arlen's usual stress levels. He'd move out of his parents' home, but he couldn't afford a one-bedroom apartment, and he couldn't toast bread if his life depended on it.

Daily life survival skills? He'd missed that lesson in school.

He turned the key and listened to the car come alive. Thoughts of Darcy, Efrain's nervous guy-to-guy talk, and all things supernatural and linked to St. Anthony's promptly vanished under the more enticing notion of take-out food and a necessary visit to that lonely little cabin.

He knew Darcy wasn't a vegetarian, so he went straight to his favorite burger joint, ordered what he hoped would help him pull some much-needed information out of Darcy's sweet and charming head.

Arlen blinked. "Sweet and charming? Where the hell did that come from?"

He had to laugh quietly at himself as he carefully set the bag of food and the tray of drinks on a waterproof food and drinks tray he'd purchased for this very purpose. He had no idea if anyone else in the world was as fussy as he was when it came to keeping his car cleaner than a museum, but that conveniently designed plastic thing now keeping his dinner safe and in no danger of spilling had proven to be a great investment.

He turned on the radio to a classic blues station as he carefully drove through rush hour traffic in downtown Dolores. He looked forward to spending more time with Darcy, business or no. Sitting at the little dining table, wolfing down bacon cheeseburgers, fries, and ice-cold sodas while staring at Darcy across the way was yet another domestic scene Arlen found he quite liked to picture in his head.

"Wonder if this counts as a second date," he muttered. A quick glance at his reflection in the glass showed him wearing a pretty idiotic, face-splitting grin, and he wondered when that happened as he never felt it form.

Chapter 17

Arlen never responded to Darcy's frantic message, but that really shouldn't bother Darcy as much as it did. Never before had he felt so cut off from the rest of the world. So hopelessly isolated but for the company—and a temporary one, at that—of a sorcerer's familiar.

Loneliness had been his life from his birth, even his unwed mother displaying a rare and random bout of melancholy whenever she gazed out the windows. It had always been the main thread weaving his existence day in and day out, and Darcy had long grown used to it. Had learned to ignore it whenever something close to a feeling of desolation touched his heart and his mind with a mournful weight.

Now he felt trapped in that little cabin, watching the sun move above, keeping track of how the shadows gradually lengthened with the passing of time. He'd cleaned the interior from top to bottom, even cleaned the bathroom despite the fact it wasn't time for it yet. He'd taken a nap with Willie curled up on the blankets next to him, snoring and twitching.

The outside appeared as normal as ever, but Darcy still sensed a growing weight of *something* out there. A certain wrongness that he couldn't quite put a finger to, let alone name to his satisfaction.

It had been steadily creeping since his visit to the cemetery and the terrifying sight of St. Anthony's gates being flung wide open. And for some time, he kept going back and forth about whether or not this feeling was nothing more than mere fancy on his part. He eventually knew—and accepted—it was absolutely real.

Darcy had gone back to the kitchen to peer out the window and check the gates from the safety of his home, not even sure what exactly it was he was expecting to see. The gates remained wide open, the three lawn bags still lined up and untouched against the iron fence.

Willie, for his part, had settled down after perhaps an hour of non-stop pacing and restless peering out of windows. The cat had even trotted upstairs and spent a good chunk of time there, and when Darcy went up to see how things were, he found Willie stretched out on the ancient leather trunk Darcy's mother had claimed contained whatever was left of the Winter family's identity.

Old photographs barely surviving the ravages of time, random and quite useless receipts, prayer books from the more devout family members, and some other artifacts and discolored costume jewelry all crammed inside a dented and half-rusty biscuit tin. They were all nothing but random items that certainly bound generations of the Winter family together, and Darcy didn't quite know what to do with them.

Darcy himself had already gone through the contents several times in the past when he was a child. Nothing had taken a hold of his imagination, and the leather trunk remained shut and stored in the garret room for the next several years.

Other items kept in the loft were Darcy's chair and cello, a turn-of-the-century writing-desk with its own fancy little drawers and matching chair, a small wardrobe whose doors and drawers could barely be moved, and Darcy's old baby crib. He'd already gone through that writing-desk over the years, opening and closing drawers and finding them empty and disappointing.

Every piece in that room continued to enjoy Darcy's care and attention, and he spent time dusting and polishing the furniture as well as sweeping the wood floor. Even the little window on each long end of the garret was allowed some homemade curtains.

Darcy couldn't help himself, anyway. The little cabin had been with his family forever, and it was his birthright. He simply had no other world besides this place, and at least for now, that was good enough for him.

It was now half past five, and the shadows outside were gathering.

The feeling of creeping wrongness continued, the extreme subtlety of its presence proving to be far more eerie compared to a full-blown supernatural event.

Darcy marched up to the kitchen window to look out one more time. Then he jumped and screeched when a steady knocking on the front door shattered the silence.

"Mooowwr! Yoowr! Yooooooowrr!"

Willie darted out of the bedroom door straight to the front door, his howls reaching some pretty impressive levels of deafening loudness. Darcy had spun around and sagged against the counter, his heart damn near squeezing itself out of his wide open mouth.

Arlen Stroescu ambled over to the picture window of the dining room, grinned at Darcy, and waved cheerily.

"Honey, I'm home!" he called. "I brought dinner!"

"Jesus Christ on a fucking cracker," Darcy muttered as he stumbled toward the door.

Before long Arlen was striding inside, bearing a rather large bag of greasy stuff and a drink carrier. He went straight for the dining table while Darcy locked the door behind him after scanning the immediate vicinity and finding the quiet area a touch disturbing in its state of calm. It was still outside—too still. Darcy didn't need any more convincing and quickly shut and secured the door.

"Did you get my message?" he asked as he busied himself with turning the lights on and pulling all the curtains close. "I called you earlier today and left a message."

Taking dishes out of the sideboard and looking for all the world as though he were the master of the house, Arlen glanced back over his shoulder to frown at Darcy.

"Message? I didn't get any. My phone was on the whole time."

"Meeowr!" Willie cut in sullenly from where he now settled himself on the couch. Even the look he gave Arlen was accusatory.

"Well—there's nothing wrong with my phone," Darcy replied. "I also kept it on all day and even recharged it."

Arlen walked back to the dining table with the dishes and set them down, his frown deepening.

"That's downright bizarre. I've been getting messages left and right from other people. For some reason, yours never came through."

"But I was able to get your answering service. You can even check my phone if you'd like."

"No, I believe you. I just find it..." Arlen paused and glanced in Willie's direction. "Willie? You tried to talk to me, too?"

Darcy blinked and looked at Arlen. "Huh? What? You guys talk? How?"

As though in answer, Arlen fixed his razor-sharp focus on his familiar, and the two of them stared, unblinking, at each other for several seconds. Darcy then realized they were communicating with each other through some kind of connection—psychic, most likely—and he felt rather stupid for not really taking such an idea more seriously before. What else could be expected from a sorcerer and his familiar, after all?

At least Darcy knew better than to interrupt such a link while it was in use. With a sigh, he finished setting the table and distributing the food and drinks.

Arlen concluded whatever conversation he was having with Willie and turned his attention back to Darcy. He moved closer and pulled a chair out, smiling faintly as he sat Darcy down before taking his seat across the table. His gallantry didn't escape Darcy's notice, and neither did the subdued mood. Arlen seemed a touch distracted, no doubt turning a good deal of things over and over in his head, based on whatever it was Willie had told him.

Time for Darcy to chase after the sorcerer before he lost Arlen completely to his wildly and endlessly turning thoughts. Time to rein him in.

"So—let's start with the communication thing," Darcy said after another awkward moment of silence. "What happened with the phone, Arlen? Why didn't it work?"

"For the same reason Willie's communication to me didn't quite make it, either." Arlen paused and indicated the cabin with a wave of a hand. "There's a pretty thick—blanket, if you will—that's settled over the cabin, and it's been working like a—well, blanket—keeping everything in here pretty much isolated from the world outside the cabin."

"Wait, what? I'm not following you."

Arlen didn't respond right away, instead dropping his gaze to his food as he considered what to say next. Then he sighed, an air of determination in his manner now. "Something seems determined to protect you. Keep you safe—probably because you're doing it a good turn."

Darcy could only blink in confusion, his meal momentarily forgotten. "I don't get it."

"You're a really good person, Darcy. You are. You take amazing care of a cemetery everyone's forgotten. You look after those whom no one bothers to think about anymore. I don't think I've ever met anyone who was as selfless as you, even toward the dead. I mean—how many people can admit to taking on the kind of back-breaking and likely dangerous work of clearing out a ruined cemetery?"

"There are charitable organizations or places like 'Friends of Yadda, Yadda' that help out and actually put together cemetery cleaning and maintenance as a voluntary thing that people can sign up for. Those things are everywhere, I'm sure."

"Yeah, but they don't work like you, though. You didn't even have to be told or asked. You just decided to treat long-dead people with the respect they've been deprived of for so long."

Darcy scowled. "But what's that got to do with the protection magic in my cabin and all that stuff you were talking about earlier?"

A host of different expressions alternately lightened and darkened Arlen's handsome features. And if Darcy weren't so baffled by the subject of their conversation, he'd have thoroughly enjoyed watching the sorcerer's many moods and even thoughts make themselves known on his face.

It was a marvel, on the whole, considering how Darcy had long been used to seeing nothing but "resting grim face" on Arlen Stroescu. Seeing just how expressive Arlen could really be was a revelation that struck Darcy hard, and he found himself halfway mesmerized.

"Your music," Arlen replied instead. His voice had dropped to a quieter and more soothing timbre. "You play your cello sometimes. Who listens to your music?"

Darcy's breath caught, and he stared at Arlen in a moment of mute panic. No, he couldn't—shouldn't—talk about the mothers. They did nothing wrong. If Arlen or any of the sorcerer-hunters found out about his weekly audience, those poor souls would likely be purged, what miserable excuse of an identity left to them gone for good. Darcy hesitated for a moment, swallowing and pretending interest in his drink.

"N—no one. I just—I just practice b—because I want to."

"Then who are the ghosts who visit you in the loft? I think they come to listen to you play. Do you play for the dead, then? Is that how you take care of them as well?"

Darcy gaped in stunned shock at Arlen, suddenly unsure how best to answer.

"I—don't know wh—what you're talking about."

Arlen's gaze hardened a little and then softened. He didn't need to respond to an all-too-clear lie. He'd caught Darcy in his net, and that was simply that.

When a warm, furry body rubbed against his leg, drawing his attention to Willie's wide, alert eyes peering up at him from the shadows of the table, Darcy knew it was useless prevaricating.

"Okay," he said, sagging against the backrest and unable to meet Arlen's gaze. "I'll tell you everything."

Chapter 18

Arlen could barely eat his food, his attention wholly fixed on Darcy as he spoke in a soft, halting voice about his connection with a group of forgotten ghosts he called "the mothers". How Charlotte Winter had come up with the idea of playing for the dead, though as to when and how she'd gotten the idea, Darcy couldn't say.

"She was already playing for them for as long as I can remember," Darcy said, brows creased as he fought to recall. "I wish I could think back to when I was a lot younger, but my memory's kind of muddy when I do."

"Why would it matter so much?" Arlen prodded gently, reminding himself he was navigating through a sea of broken glass, and he could see just how much the efforts to recall seemed to bother Darcy.

It wasn't a normal kind of disturbance, either. From where he sat, carefully reading his dinner companion (or should he say "date"?), he could tell there was something in Darcy's distant past that nagged at him. Affected him in some way, perhaps in a way relating to his current bittersweet situation with the mothers.

"B—because I think once I remember what it is, I'd be able to understand why I'm here. Like why my mom and my whole family through the years were kind of stuck in this cabin. W—we can't leave, you know. We shouldn't, anyway."

"Why do you say that?"

Darcy shrugged, worrying his lower lip as he dropped his gaze to his nearly empty plate. Arlen's attention briefly shifted to his mouth, the shine of grease on it and giving Arlen unnecessary and unwanted images.

"It's like a curse, isn't it? I pretty much figured out it's got something to do with St. Anthony's since the mothers were buried there. I just don't understand why." Darcy paused, brows wrinkling. "No, actually—it's almost like a duty. Like it's our duty—my family's duty—to stay here and take care of St. Anthony's and the mothers."

Arlen nodded, having arrived at the same conclusion yet not wishing to entertain it further till that moment, and then urged the conversation forward.

The mothers would come to the loft—the garret room as Darcy called it—around once a week. It was always on a Sunday, which Arlen wondered had anything to do with Gregory Winter and his devout leanings. Were the mothers also churchgoing women once upon a time? Most likely, given the historical period and Dolores's rural situation, at least back then.

Was Darcy also regarded as a surrogate of God or of Gregory Winter himself?

Arlen had to shake his head and rein in his wildly spiraling ideas. He was overthinking things, a voice in the back of his mind insisted. Perhaps the answer to everything was a lot simpler than he'd always come to believe.

The idea of the Winter family somehow being bound to some unusual duty involving a forgotten cemetery, however, made a great deal more sense than anything he'd toyed with in his head. And the longer he spent time with Darcy, the more he felt he was following the correct trail of breadcrumbs.

Darcy's music varied, though he'd played a handful of songs repeatedly throughout the months whenever he didn't feel up to the task of planning things out. The mothers seemed not to mind, their presence appearing to limit itself to the music and Darcy's company.

Ghosts. Dead long, long ago. Sad ghosts. Lost and confused. Need Darcy. Can't let Darcy go.

Need Darcy. Their son. Need their son. Need something they were denied. Won't let go. Can't let go.

Arlen's breath caught at Willie's words from his initial reading of the loft not too long ago. Pieces were starting to fall into place, parts of a foggy puzzle that gradually painted a sad picture.

"It almost sounds like you're singing them a lullaby," he said, a faint smile forming. "It's—incredibly sweet. Bittersweet, really, that you're taking good care of them, making them feel wanted. Loved."

Darcy blushed furiously now, and he cleared his throat as he fumbled for whatever was left of his fries. He shrugged and spoke without meeting Arlen's gaze though Arlen desperately wished he could look into those expressive eyes—and see if he could coax another smile out of Darcy. Darcy was always so quiet and serious, and it felt as though the world was everything good and perfect whenever he broke out in that bright, guileless expression of joy.

"It's only right that I play music for them. I mean, if this is what you'd call a curse or whatever, with my family pretty much stuck here forever and ever, I think I'm okay with it. I'll give them their music."

"But it forces you into a pretty lonely existence."

"I never let that bit get to me. Honestly. I've been so used to this that it doesn't bother me."

Arlen suspected otherwise. He noted some ever so subtle squirming when Darcy replied, though it also appeared as though Darcy wasn't even aware of those revealing body movements.

The response also came a tad too quickly to be interpreted as not being too defensive. Arlen inwardly sighed, deciding he really should give Darcy much more room and space. The poor fellow was obviously in way over his head and had absolutely no idea how he should be dealing with things.

"But why this, though? Why would your great-great grandfather's actions be affecting every generation after?"

Arlen proceeded to share what he'd learned about Gregory Winter with a startled Darcy.

"I do wonder if the reason for the cemetery closing down all of a sudden was something like a backlash among people who were like him—you know, devout Catholics—but who disagreed with what he was trying to do."

"Maybe it was because he died. Did you find any cause for his death anywhere?"

Arlen shook his head. "I had to stop my research because the library was closing down, and the library guardian was getting a little too antsy and salty. But I'll get back into it first chance I can tomorrow."

Darcy now appeared stunned as he regarded Arlen from across the dinner table.

"Really? You're doing all of this for me?"

There was a breathless and disbelieving quality to Darcy's words and delivery that chipped away at Arlen's dogged resolve not to be so emotionally attached to his—subject.

No, he quickly corrected with an angry huff, not subject. Never a subject. Arlen suddenly found himself in unfamiliar waters; in fact, he'd been neck-deep in them more and more since he asked Darcy out on a date.

Yes, he was beginning to find Darcy immensely attractive, the young man's natural kindness and sweetness easily finding their way through what would be cracks in Arlen's shiny armor. Arlen had clearly underestimated Darcy's influence on him despite Darcy's lack of awareness of his effect on others—particularly a sorcerer-hunter who'd long prided himself in his razor-sharp focus and granite-like determination to get things done.

"Once a sorcerer, always a sorcerer, I guess," he blurted out when he found himself once again perilously close to the edge of sentimentalism. He needed to sound indifferent and careless. "I sensed supernatural residuals on you, and I decided then to make sure you're not in any danger from the otherworld."

"I—never had anyone ever do something like that for me. Go through all that trouble, I mean. That's—thank you."

A painfully awkward pause followed. And just like that, Darcy's surprise and pleasure melted into a moody resignation. It boggled the mind, the way their connection fluctuated so wildly in emotion from second to second. If Gloria were around to watch this sorry display, she'd surely give Arlen a massive slap upside the head. And probably pinch Darcy's cheeks to get him to behave as well.

"Well—I kind of figured out you only asked me on a date so you can get to know my history and stuff. I mean, it's okay, really," Darcy hastily added, raising a hand as though to stop Arlen from reacting to what he'd just said. "If I'm going to pose a threat to anyone even without me being aware of it, I'd rather that you—or any sorcerer-hunter who senses stuff like that on me—to take care of things. I want to help."

Arlen thinned his lips. Was this what developing a crush on someone felt like? Good lord, it made his head hurt. His dates in the past were all about having fun with someone he was physically attracted to with a magical bonus of amazing sex following. His heart had never been on the line at any time then, and he'd foolishly thought it was going to be the same now. *Especially* now, he had to append irritably, because he was technically *working* as he investigated the strange supernatural imprints all over Darcy and his home.

But when Darcy spoke, Arlen watched the sadness make itself known in his eyes again. It was a wordless acceptance of what he must believe to be his lot in life despite the fact that Darcy was still so young, and circumstances always changed. And subtle though the revelation might be, Arlen knew he did exactly what Gloria warned him not to do, though he had no one else to blame but himself for finding himself in this rabbit hole.

He'd just broken Darcy's heart.

Perhaps what was worse was the fact that Arlen, already flailing in choppy and unpredictable waters, had absolutely no idea how best to deal with this. He knew he'd wanted to do such a thing at first, aiming to disappoint Darcy and kill any hopes Darcy might have in a possible relationship between them. And yet—now that Arlen found himself in pretty much the situation he'd first wanted to be in, he saw just how horrible it was.

He cleared his throat once he regained his composure, guilt now rearing its unhappy head once he realized he must be making things even worse by acting as though he hadn't just had an earth-shattering epiphany.

"Thank you for understanding," he said, and he winced. "I don't want you to get hurt, Darcy. Or other people. I really appreciate your help. Um—did your mom keep any journals or diaries?"

"No, not really. There's a trunk upstairs where old odds and ends are kept, though."

"Oh, yeah. Willie told me he found nothing there."

Darcy's brows rose, and he turned to stare at a very indifferent-looking cat who was now sitting on the sideboard, carefully monitoring the conversation. "So that's what you were up to when I found you stretched out on the trunk, eh?"

"Yeah—I asked him to dig around, in a way. I'm sorry if that's too intrusive, but I really didn't want to play it safe, especially after seeing that ghost outside your cabin."

"It's okay. I do feel safer with Wills here." Darcy hesitated, again worrying his lower lip and again making Arlen deflate from a wave of too many improper thoughts. "Arlen—do you guys at the Arcane Institute do something like mind-reading or hypnosis?"

Arlen blinked at the sudden shift in conversation.

"I don't follow you."

"I mean—I'd like to have my memories brought out. From my early childhood, anyway. If I can only understand what happened to me way back then, maybe we can figure out what to do next."

"What happened to you," Arlen echoed, surprised. "So you do think something took place that involved you when you were little."

Darcy nodded. "See, one of the pieces I played for the mothers jarred something in me. And they responded to it way more strongly than to the other stuff I used. I think—I think it's got something to do with the subject, and I think it's got some kind of connection to what happened to me when I was a little kid. I can't just ignore it, Arlen. The effect—I mean the way the piece messed with my head was pretty strong, and it kind of left me really unsettled."

Arlen nodded, frowning. "Okay, I'll ask around."

And it seemed as though the conversation had officially come to a very awkward close, and the two finished their dinner, each lost in his own thoughts.

Chapter 19

He almost forgot to mention it, but Darcy managed to sneak in a last minute update on what had happened to him in the cemetery. Arlen took careful note of everything as usual, his manner as quiet and thoughtful as ever could be, though he did reassure Darcy he didn't believe it was anything worth losing sleep over.

"Humph. Famous last words," Darcy grumbled as he watched Arlen drive off into the night.

Tuesday came, and Darcy dared to venture out in the mid-morning with Willie in tow in order to move the lawn bags still waiting for him by the cemetery gates. He couldn't help a shudder at the sight of the entrance staying wide open, with Willie darting past him and vanishing among the weeds and vines within. Arlen had reassured him—countless times, at that—that the furry little familiar was perfectly safe and knew how to protect himself in addition to having a much-needed hexed collar for extra insurance.

"Be sure to be back in a couple of hours!" he yelled at the cat. "I'm not going to stay out here today!"

"*Yoowwwr! Yoowwwr! Mrowwr!*" Willie yelled back from somewhere, drawing a burst of laughter from Darcy.

It took him much longer than usual as he'd apparently stuffed the bags rather too much this time around, but Darcy managed to get all three back at the cabin, setting them by the side door. He'd have to call the Green Collective to pick up the bags. With any luck, that small organization of nature sorcerers would be able to make good use of the clippings for whatever spells they studied, designed, and wove.

The day dragged a bit, with Darcy finding himself aimlessly afloat with nothing really planned for the rest of his time off. He scowled at his reflection in the bathroom mirror once he finished his shower.

"God," he muttered, "am I sort of like Arlen in the workaholic department?"

What a sad statement he was making to himself, now that he considered it, that he wouldn't know what to do with himself when allowed a break from work. He might not be the most filled out person on the planet, but he'd never fallen ill for any reason in the past, at least since his adolescence. There'd been no reason for him to call in sick at work, hence the obscene amount of paid time off he'd amassed.

Why was he working so hard and so consistently, anyway, even with his inheritance? He'd convinced himself he needed to make sure the money lasted for as long as possible, but even he barely managed a feeble scratch whenever he paid for property taxes or other taxes and fees required by the city, the county, and the state. Darcy had been lucky to be the heir to a shocking fortune, yet there he was, penny-pinching and living in a tiny cabin with barely functioning appliances.

What on earth was he so afraid of?

He thought about Arlen and again reminded himself it was because he was too lonely to manage any free time that the rest of the working world would deem to be a massive blessing. He'd sooner spend every moment of his time at work, his mind too focused on Benjamin's remarkable confections and ensuring the shop succeeded. Being busy was far preferable than being alone with nothing but, literally, ghosts from the past keeping him company.

And he wondered if any of his family had ever felt the same before. If his inheritance was large, did that mean his ancestors had also taken to work to alleviate the suffocating solitude imposed on them, which would have kept the money intact or even added to with judicious budgeting?

It certainly explained—or allowed him a possible explanation—why his grandparents had decided to pack up and leave even before his mother was born. Perhaps they'd understood the family's forced role too well and had decided not to subject their children, however many they'd have, to the same fate that dogged every generation before.

Darcy sighed and shook his head as he finished combing his hair.

"Mom, I wish you kept a diary," he said. "Or kept a record from your family about our history."

Midday turned into early afternoon, mid-afternoon, and early evening. Willie had long returned home, his fur dusty and sporting random bits of dirt, though he appeared to be quite alert and rather pleased with himself as he trotted inside. Darcy had to clean him up, much to the cat's dismay, though Willie turned out to be a good sport while Darcy vigorously rubbed him down with a wet, clean rag.

He at first wanted to toss the cat into a sink full of water, but in the end, Darcy decided not to tempt fate too much. Willie might have nine lives, but he only had one.

"I can't have you napping on the bed with parts of the cemetery still on your fur, buddy," he said after he released the cat and endured a withering look before Willie strutted away with a contemptuous flick of his tail. Sure enough, Darcy found him on the bed, grooming himself and tidying up the mess of damp fur Darcy had given him.

Darcy didn't know when Arlen would be dropping by, if at all, as Arlen had never said anything when he left after dinner. When exhaustion claimed Darcy, he decided to take a nap before dinner, and he joined Willie in bed.

"Hey, what's up?" he murmured sleepily.

Willie had begun pacing around the bed after Darcy crawled under the covers, walking over Darcy a few times, but Darcy didn't sense anything of a panicked or threatening nature in the cat's behavior. Willie, if anything, seemed to be in a trance-like state, repeating movements almost indefinitely until he finally stopped. The cat appeared frozen in position, ears swiveling as though he were listening for something too faint for Darcy to hear. And then, just like that, Willie stalked over to Darcy's pillow, sitting himself directly before Darcy's face, and stared down at him.

"What?"

Willie remained silent for a few seconds, which was enough time for Darcy to feel the pull of sleep, and he went under. The last image he saw while awake was of Willie moving closer to the headboard before lying down and curling himself around Darcy's head. He felt like a warm, furry, purring hat, but something faint nudged at Darcy's fading consciousness, telling him the familiar was attempting to do something.

Comfort, Darcy thought, smiling as he went under. Comfort and companionship. Protection.

* * * *

Sweet, sweet child, come out! Play with us!

Soft growling pulled Darcy out of sleep. He blinked his eyes open and found the cabin blanketed in gathering shadows. Willie had apparently abandoned his position and now sat in the bedroom doorway, growling. Darcy immediately sat up and watched the cat, the jarring shift from rest to full wakefulness barely registering as his heart sped, and he felt his hair stand on end.

Willie wasn't looking at anything in the living room. He was looking up at the ceiling of the bedroom—at the garret room.

"Wills? Do you hear something?" Darcy whispered, not daring to raise the volume of his voice.

Willie continued to growl, but he didn't budge where he sat. He looked like a furry little sentry, alerting possible threats of his presence and daring them to try to get at Darcy. And Darcy would have snatched him off the floor and given him a tight hug had he not been frozen in growing terror.

Creak. Creak. Cree-e-eea-ak.

That sounded like an old, rusty door being forced open. One long unused and neglected. The dresser? No. The wardrobe?

Thud. Thud.

There was someone or something upstairs. It wouldn't be the mothers, Darcy knew. It was only Tuesday. But something had fallen to the floor, and as he waited, he heard the faint but distinct sounds of an object being moved across the floorboards. The movement was choppy and irregular, as though whatever was propelling the object didn't have as much energy or much of a grip on it, and it took a good deal of effort.

Just like the rusted doors he'd heard immediately before the rest of the sounds.

Slowly Darcy moved to the edge of the bed, groped for his glasses, and put them on.

"Wills," he whispered again as he stood up, his eyes wide as he tried to peer into the deepening gloom outside. "Wills, stay with me. Don't go out there."

Willie's growling continued, and he kept his attention fixed on the ceiling.

Darcy closed the distance between them, and he gently bent down to take the cat in his arms. Luckily Willie didn't panic at the contact, and he allowed himself to be handled while keeping his attention on the strange sounds above.

The light scraping sounds continued, and in the silence of the cabin and its environment, the sounds seemed to grow in volume. Darcy swallowed and inched toward the bedroom door, his gaze darting toward the front door and his mind frantically calculating just how quickly he could run to it, unlock it, and bolt right out. Of course, he'd be running into the growing evening shadows beyond, but that would be preferable to being trapped inside a small cabin with something upstairs.

Thud! Thud! Thud!

Whatever it was that was being moved across the floor above was now being pushed down the stairs. The object thudded against each step, and Darcy couldn't take it anymore.

With a garbled little cry, he dashed out into the living room, barely making out the door as he neared it. Willie's growls turned into loud hisses, and the cat started to struggle in Darcy's arms.

"Yoowwwr! Yoowwwr! Mrrreowr!"

With a final surge of furious energy, Willie slipped out of Darcy's hold, kicked off his shoulder, and flew off.

"No! Willie! Come back here! Willie!"

The terrible thudding stopped just as Darcy fumbled for the locks, and at that moment, so many things happened at the same time.

Just as Darcy managed to turn the knob, something flew across the room in his direction and struck the door just next to his feet with a loud and heavy bang. Terrified, Darcy let go of the doorknob and shrieked, jumping away from the object and losing his footing so that he fell on the floor. He didn't even register any pain though he knew he'd landed hard on his side.

His glasses tumbled off, leaving him even more vulnerable with his terrible eyesight. In the dark, his vision was worse than useless.

"Willie!" Darcy cried. "Come back here, you crazy cat!"

Somewhere in the dark, Willie howled and hissed and chased something, the furious scrabbling on the floorboards indicating a wild chase.

Darcy didn't dare look at where Arlen's familiar went.

Once the shock of his fall wore out and the dizziness faded, the horror of the moment again took over, and Darcy scrambled away from the front door and whatever lay there, breathing raggedly and wishing Arlen would come. He barely noted the sudden and sheer drop of the cabin's temperature as he struggled to put some distance between himself and whatever it was that had tried to get to him.

The sudden knocking on the front door tore another cry of panic from his throat. Darcy, functioning on automatic, turned around and tried to stumble to his feet. Apparently he'd moved too close to the sideboard in the dark without realizing it, and he struck his head hard against the heavy wood, and his cries fell silent.

Chapter 20

"The hell..."

It sounded like the end of the world taking place inside Darcy's cabin. Arlen heard a series of terrified cries, lots of feline howling and screeching, and things falling hard on the floor—possibly furniture. A mix of anger and panic kicking in, Arlen tried to force his way into the cabin with a spell, sending the door swinging wide and nearly flying off its ancient hinges.

"Darcy? Darcy!" he cried. Where the hell was the light?

Ghost here. Here. Keeping it for you. Hurry.

Where's Darcy? Wh—I see him. He's out cold. I think he hit his head or fainted.

Hurry! Can't hold it too long!

Arlen wished then he were gifted with the ability to duplicate himself, so he could tend to Darcy, who lay in a crumpled heap by the sideboard, and dash up the stairs to Willie, who'd trapped and held a ghost in the loft against its will.

Arlen dropped to his knees by Darcy, gently touching Darcy's cold face and holding it secure between his hands. He closed his eyes and worked quickly, casting a hurried healing and somnus spell on Darcy, even succumbing to the pull of impulse by sealing the spell with a kiss on the tip of Darcy's nose and then his forehead.

He gently set Darcy's head back on the floor while shutting the door with another hurriedly cast spell. Then he leapt back to his feet, darted around the corner, and thundered up the stairs.

In the meantime, the hexed lights turned on as though triggered by a timer, flooding the cabin's interior with weak illumination, but that was enough for Arlen's purpose. Soon he found himself standing at the top of the stairs, staring in amazement at the hunched, swaying figure of the same ghost he'd seen and chased just a couple or so nights ago.

The ghost stood before an ancient wardrobe whose doors stood wide open and all its drawers pulled out. A pretty typical sight of a piece of furniture affected or touched by something from the otherworld, calling to mind too many horror films that had made use of such an image.

For this particular moment, however, Arlen sensed something less ominous about the darkly dream-like tableau before him. A quiet ripple of mourning and desolation moved through Arlen, a very, very faint echo of a long-muffled emotion, which forced him to stop and re-center himself even as his mind fought to make sense of what was now unfolding.

Willie looked like a stalking predator frozen in position, his body stiff and low to the ground, his growls barely heard. The ghost regarded Arlen from where it stood, its presence inside an old and rustic loft lending a ghoulish surrealism to the picture. Willie's combined power with Arlen's as a familiar had locked the ghost in place, and with Arlen joining him physically, the magic increased.

A shudder wracked Arlen's body at the sight of the ghost—a dead man's phantasm caught in a state of decay or mummification. The skeletal "limbs" showing under the tattered shroud twitched and flexed against the constraints of light magic.

"Who are you?" Arlen demanded. "What are you doing here? What do you want from Darcy?"

The ghost merely regarded him for a second or two, shocking Arlen further with a faint but palpable essence of human intelligence. Residual, most likely, but still somehow able to understand and respond. Even with both of its eyes shut, it still managed to give such an eerie impression.

Perhaps even more surprising was the fact that the ghost never once gave off even a hint of a threat to Arlen now that they were closed in like this. If anything, the more Arlen attempted to push past the thick, invisible cloak of *nothingness* surrounding the ghost, he swore he could feel a lingering sadness coming from old, forgotten places in its former being.

No, Arlen realized, this ghost wasn't a danger to anyone. It seemed—its behavior, in fact, felt more like a desperate effort at reaching out. But to whom? Darcy?

"No," Arlen whispered as piece after shadowy puzzle piece began to fall into place. "No, you weren't reaching out to him, were you? It was me. You—knew—sensed—me being a sorcerer. Is that right?" When the ghost didn't respond with a sound or a movement, Arlen decided to continue chasing after the thought. "You never showed yourself to Darcy, but to me. I think you felt me more when I hung around Darcy and not when I'm out there, watching his cabin on my own. I know who you are now."

A moment of eerie, hollow silence followed.

"Like Darcy's a conduit, right? By blood. He's your descendant. I only watched him from a distance, and you didn't reach out for me. Or maybe you couldn't. But we dated—made an emotional connection—and now, when we're together, you sense my magic through him, and that's why you've been trying so hard to get my attention. I know you wanted me to follow you back to the cemetery, but I lost you that time." And now they were back together in one place, forging a peculiar connection. Arlen took a deep breath as confidence returned. "What can I do for you, sir?"

As though finally deciding on something, the apparition raised both hands out to Arlen. An invitation, he realized, to come closer.

Willie continued to keep watch over the proceedings, his body still frozen in place, but his growls had subsided. Arlen had to step over the cat, moving like a man completely under a spell, and before he knew what he was doing, he'd raised his own hands and felt them held by a pair of bony, icy ones.

The ghost didn't speak at all. It simply had no means of verbally communicating, but the joined hands did enough. As Arlen stared into the dead, misshapen features, he felt not terror or horror but pity suddenly coursing through him. This, he knew, had been a living man once. A man who was someone's son, someone's friend, one who grew up, felt the sadness, anger, and joy that Arlen had felt, who meant something to more than one person in his lifetime. He'd once been someone who had dreams, hopes, heartbreak, nightmares, and love.

But now he'd been trapped in this form somehow, forced to linger in a long-abandoned cemetery for reasons Arlen was determined to discover that evening.

The ghost tipped its head a little to the side in a show of curiosity or interest, perhaps, as though it had heard or felt all those thoughts and emotions coursing through Arlen. It was, in fact, a very human move, and pity for the ghost surged again.

"Tell me your story," Arlen said in as gentle and quiet a voice as he could. "I want to understand and help."

The ghost released one of his hands and pointed at the floor. Arlen blinked as he followed its shriveled and white finger. When he looked up again, the ghost made a couple of emphatic points directed at the floor while giving his other hand a brief but meaningful squeeze. Arlen managed not to wince from the feeling of dried skin, tissue, and bone contracting around his hand.

"What do you mean? The floor? What's on the..." The bulb lit. "Downstairs? Is that it?"

The ghost made a slight bow of its head, the movement stiff and difficult to watch. It only added to the wave of pity that once again assailed Arlen. The lingering sadness also found a way to Arlen's consciousness, but its touch was fleeting and gone too soon. Arlen managed to recognize it, however; it was the same kind of sadness he'd seen in Darcy's eyes.

It was a sadness that was unusually specific in its context—the sadness of loneliness, of forced solitude, of being forgotten by the rest of the world even when there were still people around who'd long established connections of friendship, acquaintanceship, or what have you, with the one suffering in silence. A sadness inherited through the years, one forced onto each succeeding generation, and all because of one man's refusal to allow some of society's outcasts further rejection in death.

Book! It gave Darcy a book!

A glance behind him revealed Willie now sitting quite casually and watching the proceedings with a light of keen interest in his bright, intelligent eyes. Gone was the earlier attitude of furious defensiveness on Darcy's behalf. Like Arlen, the cat had seen into the ghost, had read it correctly as something that didn't pose a danger to anyone.

"A book? What book?"

The ghost squeezed his hand again, pointed at the floor again, and nodded again.

"I'll read it. I promise. I guess that's where I'll find all of my answers?"

The ghost nodded again, this time pointing at something behind Arlen. He hesitated when he felt the sudden and drastic change in temperatures, the sharp drop making his breaths come out in soft, cloudy puffs. Just behind him, Willie meowed. It was a soft sound, a soothing one.

Darcy's mothers are here.

Arlen braced himself and gave the ghost one final look of, hopefully, reassurance before releasing its hand and turning around. His breath caught in his throat at the sight of several ghosts—women, obviously—all in skeleton form, though some still had bits of dried tissue or skin barely clinging to their bones, and some had brittle strings of hair hanging down in scanty clumps from their skulls. All were still dressed even if their burial clothes were tattered, filthy, and faded. He thought he spotted at least a couple holding rotting dolls in their arms.

The group crept forward, chittering and chirping, their soft squeaks and clicks barely rending the calm of the loft. Willie had been correct, Arlen immediately saw. None of the mothers posed a threat. He took a deep breath and focused, centering his mind and reaching deeper inside him for the magic that he believed would help him.

For the next moment or so, time and the world seemed to stop, and Arlen merely stood there and looked at the mothers while they looked back at him. And it also seemed, ridiculously, that he was somehow being measured by a gang of old-fashioned chaperones wary of his intentions toward Darcy. Arlen would have laughed if he could, but he didn't even though the bizarre idea...

Well, it fit, somehow.

If Willie's initial readings of the mothers' residual impressions were correct—and Arlen had no reason to doubt his familiar's conclusions based on his own unexpected adventures in the loft—they were all there for Darcy. His own set of surrogate mothers, in a sense, another thought that allowed Arlen to weave more threads into a darkly complex tapestry of loss and yearning.

They'd been denied their own motherhood while alive. They'd been unwed mothers for whatever reason, dying in childbirth, their babies most likely dying with them. How many had stillborn infants? How many died while their children lived? No one knew, and no one would ever know.

Rejected and forgotten, they'd been forced to linger in the world of mortals as faceless, voiceless, nameless ghosts who'd somehow taken to a young man and had developed a special, otherworldly bond with him. He was their child. He was their guardian. He was their melodic angel who soothed them with sweet music from his cello. He'd welcomed them just as his mother had before him.

And there was Charlotte Winter as well—yet another unwed mother but one who'd turned out more fortunate than her predecessors in this shadow-laced universe of theirs. She'd understood their grief. She'd felt their pain. Whether or not her role as the mothers' adopted daughter or their fellow-"sinner" had been forced on her, the fact was that she and her one and only child had shown a great deal of humanity and mercy toward people they never knew. And would never know about, even when finally on the other side of the veil separating two worlds.

"What can I do for you?" he asked once he found his voice. Even in his own ears, he sounded terribly young and awed.

The mothers appeared to hesitate at first, and then they crept forward again, this time moving closer and closer to Arlen. Willie let out a few more quiet meows, and from behind him, the shrouded ghost—Gregory Winter, Arlen was now quite sure—pressed a cold, dead hand on Arlen's shoulder. And like a father giving his child's suitor his blessing, the ghost patted him. Arlen would figure things out soon enough, the ghost seemed to say.

Time then appeared to slow. The mothers turned around and withdrew, their crooked and misshapen forms gradually vanishing in the wood, and the night was once again restored.

Chapter 21

"Hey. Darcy, you okay, man?"

Darcy let out a little whimper as he slowly and painfully rose from the depths of unconsciousness to the hushed and careful prodding of a familiar voice. He blinked his eyes open, squinted into the dim light, and knuckled the residual fog of sleep and dreams from his head.

He found himself lying in bed, comfortably tucked under blankets, the night possibly quite late. Slight movement off to the right drew his attention, and he took in the surprising presence of Benjamin sitting quietly on a chair.

"Ben? What're you doing here?" he stammered, blinking again and gazing around him as he fought to remember what happened. "Ow. My head hurts."

"You'll be okay. You've just had a couple of ass-kicking sorcerer-hunters zapping you with healing spells. I'm sure it feels way worse now, but you're mending." Benjamin grinned and leaned forward to give Darcy's arm lying closest to him a friendly and reassuring squeeze. "Just rest. They'll be back soon."

"What time is it? And why the hell is everyone suddenly here? Sorry, no offense, boss."

Benjamin chuckled. "No worries, man. I'll let Arlen explain everything to you when they come back from St. Anthony's. I got called in for temporary nursing duty—you know, just to make sure you wake up all nice and rested. Then I'll go back home."

When Darcy opened his mouth to blurt out a horrified apology, Benjamin raised a hand to silence him. "I'd just closed the shop when Gloria and that freaky-ass bird of hers stopped by and recruited me. She'll be dropping me off at the shop once she gets back. I'm glad I get to see how you're doing, so don't worry about getting my ass dragged into your supernatural drama."

Darcy could only shake his head and offer a weak smile. "Thank you. I really appreciate it."

"How was your sleep? Seems like you had some pretty freaky dreams. Or nightmares, I guess."

"What do you mean? Oh, God, did I talk a lot in my sleep? Did I make weird noises and stuff?"

Benjamin didn't answer right away and in fact turned his gaze to another point in the room as he considered what to say. He rubbed the smooth skin of his bald head thoughtfully before letting out a deep sigh.

"Well—let me just say you were dreaming about a group of ghosts calling you outside and almost taking you away? Something like that. And also something about your mom fighting someone over you."

Darcy frowned at him, his brain whirling. "I don't..."

A sudden flash, a massive wave of dark, horrifying images and gloomy color, a confused mix of voices raised in panic, doubt, and a little boy's sobs...

"Oh, my God—Arlen? Arlen!" Darcy sat up, wide-eyed and nauseated as memories surged up and out from the darkest and deepest corners of his mind. "I—I remember!"

And he did—after years of suppression and forgetfulness, the particulars behind that fact still a vague question mark. Was Darcy hexed into forgetting a terrifying moment?

No, his mother wouldn't have had that done to him. She'd often expressed ambivalence toward the efficacy of healing magic or any spell affecting a person's biological functions. Charlotte Winter might have been a very romantic woman whose big heart at times overshadowed reason, but she'd still clung to the more pragmatic ways of science and side-eyed its less logical cousin.

"What? You remember what?"

"I—something that happened to me a long time ago. Until now, I couldn't bring it up—couldn't remember anything about it except for weird, residual feelings and stuff. Nothing solid, you know, just—echoes of feelings, I guess."

Benjamin nodded, frowning. "Go on."

Darcy had been no more than four or five. He was sleeping in the garret room, snug in bed, when he heard voices in the distance calling. He was too young to know for sure if they were saying his name, but the urge to heed the voices was too strong to ignore. Darcy, wide awake now, slid off his bed in the garret room and tiptoed downstairs, wide-eyed and careful as he picked his way through the darkness. In her bedroom his mother slept.

As he neared the door, he wondered how he was going to be able to reach the locks, but he found it quietly opening a couple of inches. As though, in fact, someone stood outside and heard him creep closer to the exit. The gap had been just enough for Darcy to widen it and slip through, shutting the door behind him and then turning his attention in the direction of the cemetery.

He'd never been afraid of St. Anthony's despite knowing what it was. The night sky was clear, the moon large and full, blanketing the ground and surrounding trees with enough light to encourage a quick exploration. Darcy didn't know why he wanted to seek out the voices. They continued to call out, a confusing collection of female sounds that didn't make any sense to him.

He hurried onward, his bare feet hardly feeling the grass and pebbles and the packed earth. The voices came from the trees skirting one side of the old cemetery. The moonlight spilled over the trees and between them, revealing a huddled group beckoning to him. Darcy, still moving without real thought, ran toward the trees.

As he neared, he saw a small group of women smiling at him and waving him over, a few of them holding up dolls. They all dressed oddly—in gowns and strange dresses that looked like nothing his mother wore. Or any woman he'd seen anywhere, anyway. But their white faces seemed to glow with love and joy, their eyes bright with tears, as though they were seeing a little boy for the first time in their lives.

"Come play with us!"

"We have nursery tales for you!"

They kept their calls, their voices light and sweet and friendly. Loving. Motherly. So Darcy went to them, and as he reached the group, they all swarmed around him and picked him up, laughing and embracing him, passing him around and kissing his cheeks and forehead with cold lips. He laughed and kicked and squirmed, delighting in the attention of those women.

"You're so beautiful!"

"Will you embrace me again?"

Then the magic wore off as Darcy's mother called his name—a frightened voice rising over the laughter. Everyone then stopped in mute surprise, shrank back into the shadows, with Darcy held fast in someone's arms.

"Mommy? Mommy?" he called out, confused, though he didn't fight against the hold or the icy lips that kept pressing kisses against his cheeks. He had to strain to catch sight of his mother beyond the shadows of the trees.

"Darcy? Where are you, honey? I'm coming!" his mother called breathlessly. "I'm coming!"

His mother eventually stumbled into view, her flushed features creased with anger as she raised one hand, revealing a shimmering rope that was visible when the moonlight touched it but vanished completely in the shadows. And, apparently, the other end was secured around his waist, though he couldn't see it at all, let alone feel it.

A guiding thread, she'd called it. An enchanted string that she'd purchased for Darcy because she'd heard the mothers' calls for him several times already, and she'd caught him trying to escape the cabin every time. The string kept him to her. Kept him from being carried off into the night by a group of dead women yearning for the children they'd been deprived of.

They wanted Darcy. They needed him. But for his mother's intervention, he would have been lost to the world forever. And just when she reached the edge of the trees, defiance in her manner as she continued to hold the guiding thread at her side, the mothers shed their forms and appeared as the ghosts they truly were. Darcy, held against the chest of a skeleton in a soiled shroud, started wailing and sobbing in terror.

"What happened?" Benjamin's soft voice prodded when Darcy fell silent, his face buried in his hands.

"They let me go," Darcy replied, overcome, his voice slightly muffled as he struggled with his emotions. "They sort of panicked when I started crying for Mom, and they let me go. I ran to her, and she picked me up, but she didn't leave right away. I think—no, I know for sure—she talked to them. Said something about them wanting something they couldn't have and how sorry she was about that. That, you know, she understood how they must feel because she's read their stories and knew about their lives. That was when she promised they can still see me as long as Mom was around to keep an eye on me. That was also when she got this idea of playing music for them—because—because that was really all she could give them that made them happy. They couldn't get me for themselves, so they settled for the next best thing, I guess, as long as they could visit me."

Darcy paused to gather himself, dashing the tears away with a clumsy swipe of his hand. "And you know what? They listened. The mothers listened. And they went with it. I'm sure it's because they really didn't have a choice. They're kind of trapped here—couldn't move on for some reason. Or maybe they weren't allowed to. But—they never hurt me after my mom faced off with them, you know? Even after she died, they never hurt me or never tried to take me away again like before. They kept their end of the deal, and I made sure to keep mine—or my mom's."

Perhaps it was a shade of their humanity showing itself, after all. That they'd understood and had resigned themselves to the fact that Darcy belonged in the world of the living, that he was nothing more than a representative of what they'd lost. That, maybe, they'd understood the nature of the crime they'd almost committed by trying to carry Darcy away while still alive. Who could really say, though? At least Darcy knew that several aspects of his life would forever be shrouded in mystery, and he would simply have to live with that.

Darcy didn't feel Benjamin move from the chair and sit next to him on the bed till his friend looped an arm around his shoulders and gave him a comforting half-embrace. Benjamin didn't have to speak. His steady, quiet presence and non-judgmental ear were enough for Darcy to compose himself if only for the moment.

"So if your mom didn't make that promise and just ran off with you, they would've come back again and again till they got what they wanted," Benjamin offered after a moment's silence.

Darcy nodded against his friend's shoulder. "Yeah. I'd be dead, I'm sure."

Benjamin sighed loudly. "I'm glad your mom was sharp as a tack. I wouldn't have thought of using that guiding thread hex-y thing and then come up with a compromise."

"Did Arlen and Gloria tell you what's been happening here? I mean, what—like what's been going on with me and the—the mothers?"

"Yeah. They did. Goddamn scary, whatever's happening, but considering your mom didn't practice magic and managed to keep you safe with music, I say it's pretty impressive what she'd managed to pull off."

Darcy wondered if she'd tried to leave with him after such a terrifying episode. But with no signs of a journal anywhere detailing her own accounts of her dealings with those poor, unhappy souls, there was simply no way of knowing for sure. Her attempts, if any, at further saving Darcy would forever remain lost.

Money wouldn't have been an object, considering their barely touched wealth, so perhaps it had been nothing but pure sympathy and a blood connection to the man who'd set the Winter family down a dusky path that had kept her tied to the cabin and its ghosts. And she'd never spoken in earnest about the mothers, only that they needed occasional attention with music until the time came when they wouldn't. On that account, she'd been cryptic as well.

Darcy, for his part, had long been so used to playing music for them that he somehow couldn't imagine not doing it anymore. Whether or not his mother referred to death—both hers and his, eventually—Darcy figured his own death would likely mark the end of those nameless mothers' music. He was the last of his line, after all, and he was alone.

"I miss her."

"I know you do, buddy. I know you do."

And so, Darcy realized, his strange and inexplicable reaction to Schubert's *Erlkönig* now made sense. The original ballad had been about a father's desperate attempt at keeping his child from being taken by the Erl-king and his daughters. Those terrifying supernatural creatures called out to the child, tempting him with sweetened promises, which the boy kept telling his panicked father as they rode into the night. But the ballad, unlike real life, was cursed with a tragic ending, the child dying in his father's arms because his soul had been claimed.

Darcy's near-brush with death as a little boy, in a way, was the ballad corrected by his mother.

Chapter 22

It is a curse to be forgotten entirely. To be rejected, despised, reduced to nothing while one still breathes, let alone when one dies. I have forgiven my father, whoever he might have been, long ago. I have worked thrice as hard as my peers because of my disadvantage. I am proud of my wealth, my standing. I may be a bastard son in the eyes of many, but my money and faith protect me, and I am allowed to care for those women who have fallen afoul of the Church. My poor mother, just like my unhappy sleepers, suffered much, a weak, sickly thing who would have survived had she not been ignored and despised by those who should have done better by her.

I suspect my own death will be treated with as much "respect" as my unfortunate ladies. Everyone who is someone has long made their opinions known to me. I expect to be interred in St. Anthony's where I will take my place among my forgotten mothers. My final resting-place is now there, empty and waiting for me. I do not expect to wait too long for my time.

I have already felt the prayer-spell of forgetting take a hold of me. It is a chilly, insidious influence, eating its way through my skin and seeking a way to the deepest and darkest corners of my soul, ensuring my complete vanishing from all knowledge. Even my descendants'.

If my suspicions prove to be correct, I mourn for my bloodline, as I understand a prayer-spell of forgetting will work like a curse to all who follow me. Generation after generation forced into the barest semblance of a family, quite likely a parent (perhaps both if fortune wills it) and one child. No one will know what, why, who, and how their fate—a horribly lonely and limited one, at that—could be bound so tightly with St. Anthony's. If our ghosts haunt these parts, it is only because we seek compassion from those who choose to listen to us.

Compassion, understanding, forgiveness, love. Love above all. Such an easy word to throw around but terribly difficult in practice.

This curse—and I willingly call it as such—will end someday. Of that I am sure. My bloodline will not last so long. With each generation stunted in number, I suspect those who have hexed me with that prayer-spell of forgetting will have their triumph when the last of my descendants passes away, and my ladies and I are left in the shadows of St. Anthony's trees. Lost forever to the world. Nameless, uprooted, and trapped in a world that will never know of us.

I regret nothing. I forgive those who have spun this curse. And at the very least, even in death, I am still able to look after those who have lost far more than their names.

* * * *

Arlen, Gloria, and Efrain stood around the crumbling old vault, each channeling their magic and synching it with the others'. Somewhere in the cemetery their familiars wandered, alert and on guard. Globes of light danced around St. Anthony's, all cast by the three sorcerers in a bid to bring life and hope to a forgotten and dilapidated corner of Dolores.

Arlen, who stood directly before the vault's entrance, read aloud the names of the women buried in the cemetery. He used the notes he'd taken during his research, pleased to have his efforts bear some much-needed fruit. After each name, which Gloria and Efrain echoed, Arlen blessed the unfortunate woman with a prayer-spell for release and healing from St. Rafael and eternal peace in the arms of Nature herself, their tired souls guided along by Hecate's ghostly pack.

He didn't need to look around him to know what was happening in answer to his blessings. He could feel each woman rise from her grave with a shuddering sigh at the mention of her name, the sounds of Hecate's invisible hounds snuffling and waiting breaking through the gentle and tentative exhalations.

"Lizzie Hendrickson," he said, feeling an oddly hollow kind of relief in his chest at the mention of the twelfth and last mother. He blessed Lizzie and then heard her free herself of her overgrown grave.

"Gregory Winter," he said, this time walking down the stone steps and pressing a hand against the moldy bricks of the vault's sealed entrance.

He could sense movement within, which was immediately followed by a loud, pained exhalation—very likely the same sound Darcy had heard the last time he was in the cemetery. It was, as far as Arlen could read it, an expression of extreme fatigue, this time clearly edged with relief at finally, finally being freed.

Arlen blessed the soul of Gregory Winter, his prayer-spell a touch longer because of the fact that Winter had been the primary target of the prayer-spell of forgetting. He could barely keep his own emotions in check, shock and horror coming only second to grief.

Arlen was one of the more successful sorcerer-hunters around, but he'd never allowed himself to be so emotionally affected by any of his cases. All those ghosts he'd managed to send back to the otherworld were just trapped, unhappy spirits who hadn't been around long enough to be twisted and turned malignant. In fact, he'd never encountered any ghost that had dangerous energies in its makeup. Every one of them had been lost and simply needed help crossing over.

This case, however, had become personal.

And it was because there was nothing about it that required a massive supernatural showdown of some kind—no huge battle between light and dark magic. No colorful light shows when sorcerers and otherworldly forces went head to head.

No, this had all been about simple human compassion. Empathy. And, as Winter himself had indicated in his writing, love. He, his mother, and the mothers he'd served by offering them a dignified burial had been judged and found lacking based on moral standards that had always been vulnerable to arbitrariness.

Vulnerable to the whims of human nature.

And Arlen's heart broke for them and for the innocent members of Winter's family generation after generation.

Arlen took a deep breath and pulled his hand away, giving the weathered brick a final look before turning around and ascending the steps. Once he reached the top, he paused, gazing around him in amazement.

There they all were—the mothers. Barely visible, their spectral forms softly embraced by the moonlight as they stood by their respective gravestones in their original forms, regarding him with surprise and gratitude. All young, most likely in their early twenties, with perhaps three of them pitifully only in their teens, Arlen realized, his throat tightening.

He spotted those who'd appeared in the loft holding rotting dolls, though at that moment, even the dolls looked new and whole. The significance of those old toys' presence in the protective grasp of long-lost young mothers wasn't lost on Arlen, and he had to fight back his own tears at the sight.

If only he knew their stories in full because despite his efforts at freeing them, he felt that he still fell short in giving them their desperately needed rest. They were still forgotten in some way, and he thought it wasn't fair.

"Help us remember you," he stammered, breathless. And he knew immediately it was a vain plea.

The one standing nearest to him seemed to understand, and she offered him a somewhat apologetic smile and a tired shake of her head.

It was an impulsive, quiet outburst, and Arlen suddenly felt as though he were a little boy again, uncertain and confused about the workings of the world around him. A gentle pressure against his arm stopped him, however, as Gregory Winter's ghost moved past him, having finally emerged whole from his vault.

Winter had given Arlen's arm a squeeze—reassurance or gratitude, perhaps—and as the ghost walked past, he glanced back and smiled faintly, even inclining his head in a stately bow of sorts. Then Winter moved off to join his ladies, taking his place next to one of them. The mothers moved closer, surrounding him with smiles of gratitude and voiceless expressions of thanks.

They certainly looked like a dozen young daughters swarming around their doting father.

Even in death, Gregory Winter carried himself with dignity and pride, his head held high and his posture straight. Dressed in Victorian high fashion of his time, he was very much the privileged gentleman who'd star prominently in countless romances.

No, Winter had nothing to be ashamed of, Arlen thought, once again blinking away the gathering tears. He might have suffered the stigma of being a bastard child back then, but he'd risen above all that, even ensuring that his own descendants would never be in want of anything by blessing them with his hard-earned wealth.

Darcy surely would know about his inheritance, Arlen thought, but that point was nowhere near in importance as Arlen's current task. And he continued to marvel at Gregory Winter and his remarkable history.

Perhaps the best thing of all was the fact that this man had never forgotten those who were less fortunate, even forgave those who'd wronged him and his family. He'd tried what he could to honor his beloved mother, however indirectly, by taking care of those like her. And if Arlen and other sorcerer-hunters had failed in their reading of those supernatural imprints surrounding Darcy and his home, it had everything to do with the prayer-spell that had become the Winter family's curse.

Hecate's hounds began to howl, one dog following another till St. Anthony's was filled with their mournful cries. The ghosts turned away casually in a group, their attention now wholly fixed on each other and what lay ahead, the world of mortals finally a memory to them. In the middle strode Gregory Winter—still keeping a loving watch over his young mothers, still taking great care of them as he herded them all into the night.

Slowly they moved into the trees, faded, and then disappeared entirely, and immediately following that, the rush of icy winds as the hounds ran off into the night and toward their mistress's kingdom. Their baying gradually fell silent as they escorted the long-forgotten dead out of the world of the living and into the endless night.

No one moved or spoke for a long moment, waiting instead for ordinary night sounds to resume. The globes of light vanished one by one till only three were left—one for each sorcerer-hunter.

"I guess it's over," Arlen said as he spotted Efrain appear from around the corner of the vault to his left. "Let's go home."

Gloria emerged from the right, Benitez perched on her shoulder while Willie and Oliver, Efrain's familiar, bounded out of the weeds and headed straight for their sorcerers. Arlen sighed and picked up Willie, giving his cat a quick kiss between the ears.

"What're you going to do with the letter you found?" Efrain asked. He approached Arlen with Oliver held against his chest, purring loudly.

"It's Darcy's. He'll have to keep it. If not, I can submit it to the Arcane Institute for the archives."

It was really one of several letters Gregory Winter had written, all of them addressed to his future descendants. Those letters had been carefully tucked among the pages of an old, old child's nursery book, which, in turn, had been hidden in the recesses of that wardrobe in Darcy's loft. Winter had forced the contents out, drawing on what little energy he had as a ghost to force doors and drawers open, retrieve the book, and somehow get it to Darcy. Arlen suspected that Winter, having reassured himself of catching Arlen's attention, was determined to get his message across through that collection of childhood tales.

Yes, he and the mothers needed help crossing over. They'd been forced into one world for too long, serving a punishment that was worse than unjust and cruel. And it appeared as though Winter had also known—had predicted it, even—that Darcy would be the end of the line for his bloodline. It was therefore necessary to gain the attention of a sorcerer for help in shedding the prayer-spell of forgetting and being granted the peace and rest so long denied them.

"You okay, hon?" Gloria asked, brows creased with worry.

"Yeah. I am." Arlen took another deep breath. "This'll stay with me forever, but—yeah. I'm okay."

He smiled at his friend and led the way out. The letters he'd found tucked away in the pages of an old fairy tale book were practically relics and would barely survive further handling. But in that careful, stylized, cursive handwriting lay the answer to a mystery that had turned out to be far, far simpler than what Arlen had first believed.

And for that it had become precious, a unique offering to the last of the bloodline. Darcy would surely treasure his ancestor's sincere, heartbreaking accounts, an idealist's heart laid bare and tucked among the pages of a child's fairy tale book—Arlen couldn't think of a more suitable picture.

Chapter 23

The chocolate shop swarmed with customers, with autumn now in full swing, and people were getting ready for the holidays. Benjamin was beside himself despite the stress of keeping up with sales, and he'd strutted around, crowing about not needing any "special hex-y juju" to make money from his recipes. Zoe made at least two dashes to the coffee shop next door for "refills" of her caffeine cocktails and even treated Benjamin and Darcy to large servings of their favorite coffee drinks.

By closing time, they'd run out of at least four flavors and were dangerously low on six.

Darcy could barely stand as he went about his usual job of cleaning the counters and the glass display cases while Zoe washed trays in the back.

It had been almost a month since the mothers' and Gregory Winter's release. Darcy's life had gone back to nearly normal, his Sunday evenings now quiet and—lonelier. He continued to play his cello in the garret room, and he hoped the music somehow reached the mothers, wherever they were. And if so, he also hoped the music still gave them comfort.

One thing he'd also started to do was to play for Gregory Winter as well. No, Darcy wouldn't preface his music with a vocalized acknowledgement of anyone. He played his cello with specific individuals in mind. He'd managed to get the list of names from Arlen, and he took care to keep the list safe, so that he could refer to it whenever he played.

Every name would be acknowledged with music, every life, every dream and hope, though lost a long time ago. And Darcy quite liked the notion that he was instrumental in immortalizing those forgotten souls despite the heavier weight of loneliness now bearing down on him.

"So how're things coming along now?"

Darcy glanced up to find Benjamin watching him from the other side of the counter, that day's accounting piled up before him, all ready to be calculated to death.

"Um—good. It's been pretty quiet around the cabin," Darcy replied, shrugging and laughing a little awkwardly. "I think I need to get a new hobby."

"You still clean up St. Anthony's?"

"Yeah. Why shouldn't I? Just because they're all gone now doesn't mean I can just let things go."

Benjamin nodded, pursing his lips as he mulled over things. "Have you thought about moving out?"

"And go where? That cabin's my home. I inherited it, and I'm not paying a mortgage. I'm comfortable there, and I'm used to it." Darcy cleared his throat and dropped his gaze to the rag he held. He started wiping down the counter by the cash register, a touch distracted. "Arlen beefed up the protection hexes on it, you know. Also—also the lights—the electricity, I mean. He also kind of tweaked the spell on them."

"Oh, yeah?"

"Yeah," Darcy stammered, unable to meet Benjamin's gaze now as he directed his attention to another area he'd already cleaned and started wiping it down as well. "I guess now it's just—you know—a matter of upgrading stuff inside the cabin. Like—like get a new stove or maybe replace the couch or something. I was—was thinking of doing something about the garret room. M—maybe turn it into a music room or a library. Something like that."

Benjamin sighed. "What did Arlen do to the letters?"

"Oh. Um—I donated it to the Arcane Institute. Didn't I mention that? Yeah, I did. Um—I want it to be part of the archives there, so they can use it as part of their studies. You know, since I can be something like a case study for them to do more research on. I mean—I don't think I've ever heard of a prayer-spell of forgetting."

When Benjamin didn't speak, Darcy dared a look and found his employer staring at him with an incredulous frown.

"Case study? Are you fucking serious? That's all you are to them?"

"Well—what happened to me and my family kind of is, right? That's why Arlen asked me out in the first place, isn't it?"

"Has Arlen been talking to you since that night, dude? Has he visited you at all?"

Darcy hesitated, unable to come up with something careless and dismissive. He couldn't lie if his life depended on it, and he was always far too slow when it came to feigning disinterest or even glibness.

"Your silence pretty much answers my questions. Son of a bitch, that..."

"Benjamin, he's been busy, okay? And—and I kind of told him I'm not—you know—available. Or not interested."

"Wait, what? Not available? Not interested? Are you nuts?" Benjamin paused in mid-tirade. "All right, never mind. Life is nuts, period. Ghosts, magic, curses, freaky-ass birds, sorcerers—yeah, your invisible love life's nowhere near the levels of crazy of ordinary, day-to-day shit here in Dolores. I'll be in the office, crunching numbers. Make sure you lock the door when you leave."

Darcy nodded and gave his slightly frazzled employer a sheepish half-smile. Benjamin merely glared at him and then turned around to vanish through the rear doors.

"Do you need a ride home?" Benjamin called out.

"No, I'm good, thanks!"

"If you don't need a ride home and you told Arlen you're not available, it means you're seeing someone, right?" Benjamin's voice was a little more muffled now, and Darcy had to stifle a little giggle as he finished cleaning up.

"Get your nose out of my invisible love life," he hollered back. "I'll talk about it when I'm good and ready."

"Yeah, sure you will!"

"I will!"

Benjamin let out a sound that was obnoxiously close to a resounding fart, but Darcy knew better. His boss and good friend may be a genius entrepreneur, but Benjamin was also a pretty skilled sound-effect-guy, as Zoe had always described his absurd sound arsenal.

He and Zoe left the chocolate shop at the same time, bidding each other goodbye after Zoe offered him a ride home at least a couple of times. Apparently she wasn't too convinced about him not needing one, and while it required Darcy more effort than usual to make her drop it, he managed to succeed in the end.

Then again, it helped that his actual ride was waiting for him, slouched attractively against a nearby lamppost. Zoe didn't even notice Arlen as she hurried off and vanished in the never-ending crowd of evening shoppers, leaving Darcy to stand in awkward silence for a moment. He hesitated before the shop's now locked door, shoving his hands into his coat pockets and warily observing Arlen from a relatively safe distance.

It was Arlen who broke the ice, pushing away from the lamppost and sauntering over to Darcy. Not once did he direct his gaze elsewhere, the weight of his dark eyes on Darcy effectively fixing Darcy in place. Arlen Stroescu was incredibly beautiful, Darcy thought, and no amount of swallowing or throat-clearing could make his tongue loosen. He continued to gape stupidly at Arlen as the sorcerer—again dressed in his usual classy, black ensemble—finally stopped before him, eyes probing and searching.

For what? Darcy could hardly guess.

"I know you didn't want me to bother you," Arlen said, a touch hesitant. Darcy even caught sight of a faint blush coloring his cheeks. "And I'm sorry if I'm overstepping my bounds, but I really want to see you."

"You could've just texted me or something."

Arlen shrugged. "Willie didn't mind being my messenger."

The cat appeared on Darcy's doorstep that morning, a note tied to his collar. Willie looked suitably unimpressed and a touch put out by the whole thing, really, though he certainly behaved as though he owned the cabin when a startled Darcy ushered the cat inside after plucking the note off his collar.

"Besides," Arlen continued, "you pretty much told me to back off."

"And yet you didn't."

"I'm sorry. Gloria will tell you my social skills suck."

"She's right, you know."

"Yeah. I know. Listen, would you like to have dinner with me? I mean we can talk over dinner."

Darcy didn't move—couldn't move. He turned his attention from Arlen to the shoppers walking around them, the dull ache in his chest returning as he fought to compose himself.

"Everything you need to know about my family's history is already with you, Arlen. I don't have anything else to add to your research. If you're writing a paper or something like that about what happened, you won't be able to get anything more from me. I'm just as clueless about things as before."

"Darcy, I'm not writing a paper. I'm not doing research. I'm—look at me, please."

Darcy felt a hand cradle his chin and gently turn it so that he was back to staring in wide-eyed confusion at Arlen again, this time unable to look away because Arlen kept his hold on Darcy. He could feel tears welling up as reminders of his disappointment and self-directed anger returned, sharp claws tearing away at his heart all over again.

"I want to see you again," Arlen said, his voice dropping. "Not because I need something from you. Not because I have to have information. I want to see you because, well, I want to see you. Go out on dates—real dates. But only if you're willing to give me a second chance."

Darcy blinked away the threatening tears and now stared at Arlen in incredulous silence. They were back on square one, weren't they?

"You want to date me?" he blurted out after a moment. "Are you serious?"

Arlen blinked, looked baffled for a handful of seconds, and then sighed heavily, bowing his head as his shoulders drooped.

"I deserved that. I'm so sorry. But, Darcy, even if you don't want to see me again, you can't say you don't deserve to be admired or loved. Because you do. I know I really fucked things up with us, but I want to try again and make sure to get everything right this time around. But—again, only if you're willing. I'm not going to push it. Not with you. Never with you. Because you deserve better. And..."

"Okay, okay, I'll go out with you."

Good lord, Arlen wasn't about to stop, was he? But Darcy didn't care. He saw how sincere Arlen was in his admission of guilt and especially in his desire to start over. Whatever it was about Darcy that had somehow convinced Arlen to ignore the rest of the gay population of Dolores in favor of him, Darcy had no idea. And he found he quite liked that side of Arlen revealing itself to him more and more often—a more vulnerable and uncertain side of the otherwise polished and confident, workaholic sorcerer-hunter. Arlen Stroescu had chinks in his handsome armor, and those chinks made him no less beautiful in Darcy's eyes.

No, those chinks made Arlen more human and, therefore, even more interesting and attractive in Darcy's overly biased view.

Arlen, momentarily silenced, could only bend down and press a kiss on Darcy's mouth. Darcy's first honest to goodness, "real date" kiss. One that left him floating for the rest of the night and absolutely loving a gigantic and sloppy slice of pizza in Arlen's favorite cheap pizza parlor.

Chapter 24

What a difference half a year made, Arlen told himself as he stood back and gazed around him. St. Anthony's was now quite neat-looking, the weeds having been vanquished and the vines completely gone. No, there was no guarantee the cemetery would stay as clean and tidy as it did now, but it didn't require much by way of maintenance. Darcy wasn't alone anymore in his endeavors, and Arlen was determined to keep things that way.

Gloria, Efrain, and even Benjamin would come by to help now and then, and in Efrain's case, Leander would sometimes follow. As a group of three, four, or more, they covered a lot of ground and even enjoyed the work, sometimes breaking out in song or filling the once lonely cemetery with laughter and energetic conversation. It was a far, far cry, indeed, from St. Anthony's sad past, and Arlen knew Gregory Winter and his ladies wouldn't want it any other way.

Of course, it also didn't hurt to use a touch of magic here and there—nature magic, really, that he'd commissioned from the same sorcerers who used to pick up Darcy's overly packed lawn bags. The group had managed to whip up a simple spell that Arlen could use to keep weeds and overgrowth at bay or at least at a minimum. It was still good to go out and move among the gravestones, physically taking care of those buried there.

The vault had been hexed with a cleansing and protective spell. Darcy himself had asked not to have improvements made on his ancestor's final resting place because he believed the world needed a symbolic reminder of its cruelty to the less fortunate or even to those who did good work.

Even the gravestones were left alone, though the gates were most definitely fixed. In fact, Darcy had a new gate and fence made, turning to his inheritance for some much-needed resources. On the anniversary of St. Anthony's "cleansing", Darcy and Arlen planned to place flowers on the graves as well as the vault. They'd even thought of turning it into a yearly tradition.

"It's the least we could do," Darcy had said as they rested from that day's work, tired and sweaty but feeling quite accomplished. "After everything that's happened, they deserve to be remembered."

"You've done way more than anyone can expect, sweetheart, with your music. But, yeah—I agree. Considering what was done to them, it's the least we can do."

Arlen wrapped an arm around Darcy's shoulders and gave them a squeeze while dropping a kiss on Darcy's damp hair.

Following the holidays and then spring, the pair had settled comfortably into a nice situation, with Arlen agreeing to move into the cabin with Darcy at Darcy's prodding. With the release of the ghosts of St. Anthony's, Darcy's connection to the cabin had become practical. No mortgage payments, utilities that barely made a dent on the budget, an absolutely peaceful environment far from the insane bustle of Dolores proper...

Darcy's arguments for keeping the cabin were ironclad, and Arlen knew there was no fighting his boyfriend. Not that he wanted to, really, as the charm of an isolated, rustic cabin—especially one that boasted the sweetest, kindest, and most beautiful young man Arlen had ever had the honor of knowing—had long won him over. What had been novel at first was now comfortable and necessary.

Even Arlen's long-suffering parents had to pinch themselves when they received the news. Their son finally found someone willing to put up with his utter lack of basic day-to-day life skills? Oh, glorious day, indeed. At the same time, though, Arlen thought he'd overheard his father mutter something along the lines of "God, that poor boy—should we warn him now before things get too serious and too lovey-dovey?"

That was in reference to Darcy, who, happily, remained quite oblivious to his boyfriend's parents' excessive relief at having Arlen taken off their hands.

It took the pair a month of shifting things around and surrendering others to charity before the dust finally settled. Old appliances were replaced, with Darcy looking awfully sheepish and apologetic for being a "sort of trust fund baby" and reassuring Arlen that there were no plans of turning him into a kept boy.

"Besides, I like working and keeping myself busy," Darcy admitted. "Mom didn't raise me to mooch off someone else's money."

"And my mom didn't raise no fool, either," Arlen replied, grinning in relief and moving in for a long and demanding kiss that led them both sprawled on the dirty kitchen floor, tearing each other's clothes off and having their wicked way with each other till Willie broke up their come-soaked tangling with an ir-ritated howl for his food.

Darcy's old bedroom was now Arlen's antiquated and rather charming of-fice. The loft was turned into a very spacious bedroom, where Darcy still played his cello and provided soothing background music while Arlen worked down-stairs. The living room's humble collection of books had expanded, with a cou-ple more bookcases appearing, every shelf filled. Television was still non-exis-tent, and Arlen didn't miss it at all, having been used to working so much that he simply didn't have time for that.

Books? Yes. Darcy? Absolutely. Television? No, never.

Besides, Arlen brought his computer when he moved in, and the two en-joyed an occasional streaming movie on it, especially when Arlen wasn't called on to hunt.

And Willie had the run of the place, which delighted Darcy even more. The cat even had his own cat tree in the loft, and Darcy constantly wondered if they ought to fill it with kitty toys.

"I'm actually shocked we got him that thing," Arlen said as he stood behind Darcy, wrapping his arms around Darcy's waist and resting his chin on Darcy's head as they watched Willie show off his climbing skills. "I had nothing but empty boxes before. He was pretty cool with those."

"Really? But shouldn't cats have toys like fake mice filled with catnip or something?"

"Nah. I've tried before. He only looked insulted and then took a dump in one of my shoes."

The following morning Arlen found a small cardboard box with loose flaps sitting next to the sideboard. Sure enough, Willie was curled up inside, quite dead to the world. Sitting at the table, eating his breakfast and looking terribly pleased with himself, was Darcy.

* * * *

"Hey," Darcy whispered, and Arlen felt soft lips press against his mouth.

He smiled and opened his eyes. "Yes?"

"When are we going to shop for Efrain and Leander?"

"Sweetheart, their wedding won't be for another three months."

"But we both work full-time. We'll forget, I'm sure."

Darcy's worried features filled Arlen's vision as they lay next to each other. Arlen sighed and turned on his side to face Darcy, offering gentle and soothing touches on his love's cheek.

"We won't forget. I made sure to mark the calendar with deadlines. Speaking of which, we have kind of a deadline for sleeping. Like—an hour ago or something—because we have to work in the morning. Did you forget? There's this thing called bills and food and, hopefully, a vacation and a retirement account we kind of have to keep track of. Know what I mean?"

Darcy didn't answer right away. Lying on his side and facing Arlen, the moonlight touching his face and lending it a supernatural glow that took Arlen's breath away, Darcy was simply magical.

"I can't sleep."

"Why not? The wedding?"

Darcy hesitated again, and even in the near darkness, Arlen could see the blush blooming on his cheeks. "Yeah. Among other things."

"Okay, well—are those other things pretty important?"

"Kind of. Can I share one of them with you right now? I've been thinking about it all day."

Arlen sighed and shook his head indulgently. He was plain lost when it came to his man, and there was simply no way he was going to say no to anything Darcy Winter would ask of him.

"Okay, go on. What is it?"

"I love you."

"Oh, you—come here."

Laughing softly, the two wrestled a little, with Arlen successfully managing to roll on top of Darcy and kissing his love thoroughly.

When he pulled away, he looked down at Darcy's flushed and smiling features, a wave of quiet joy coursing through him. How did he manage to get this lucky? How could life work in such a way so that not too long ago, Arlen couldn't think of anything but work, work, work, and then all of a sudden, there he was, hopelessly in love with someone he barely gave much thought to in the past?

Once in a while, Arlen wondered if his happiness now was something like a parting gift from Gregory Winter himself. The man had wondered, after all, and had given voice to his thoughts in his letters about his bloodline dying sooner than later. For Darcy to be the last in the family, being gay and unable to give birth unless it was through surrogacy if he wished for the bloodline to continue...

No, Arlen corrected himself. He'd already gone over this in his head a number of times before.

Arlen knew in his heart the ghost had seen it, recognized Darcy's crippling solitude and the threat of a future of loneliness. And that Gregory Winter had somehow been instrumental in ensuring Arlen's presence in Darcy's life even as Winter had sought out Arlen for help.

Or at the very least, Winter had taken full advantage of Arlen's interest in Darcy's life so that he got two things out of it in the end: freedom from his enemies' curse and the guarantee of happiness for his young descendant's future. Were ghosts ever that wily? Arlen could drive himself crazy mulling over such things.

Then again, Fortune herself had her own way of making things happen, and Arlen's current happiness had absolutely nothing to do with any supernatural machinations from a ghost—matchmaking efforts and otherwise.

Arlen had to sigh and shake his head at himself.

There he was, overthinking things yet again while in the grip of absolute joy and a humbling reminder of just how lucky he was that he'd be loved by someone as remarkable as Darcy Winter. No—in this case, there was simply no room for logic and reason.

Arlen felt, deeply and utterly.

And while the experience had at first been alien and pretty alarming as it left him discombobulated more often than not, Darcy had taught him to let things go, to accept, to adapt, to live, and to understand that he shouldn't be questioning things so much. Life simply didn't work so neatly and so predictably, after all. It was colorful and messy more often than not, and that was the beauty of it.

So he smiled back and kissed Darcy's nose, his chin, his forehead, while punctuating each with "I" and "love" and "you". He could do this all night if he didn't have to get up by a certain time the following morning.

"Okay, are you ready to go to sleep now?" he asked, rolling himself off and settling himself back down while tugging Darcy close. Darcy tended to fall asleep more quickly when his head rested against Arlen's shoulder. "No more hanky-panky, mister. If you want me to earn decent money, you shouldn't keep me from my work."

He could feel Darcy grinning against his skin, and Arlen rolled his eyes before shutting them.

"Don't even start with that 'kept boy' talk, Winter," Arlen blurted out. "I know you've got enough money to retire before you hit twenty-five even though you're still working full-time, but that shit ain't going to do it for me, you hear? I'll work and earn money until I'm too old to do it anymore."

Darcy was sniggering now. "Yes, boss. Boy, did I bag myself a hopeless workaholic or what?"

"Yeah, yeah. Okay. Good night. Or good morning. Go to sleep, you nut."

Darcy yawned and pressed a kiss against Arlen's chest before snuggling even closer. "Good morning."

Don't miss out!

Visit the website below and you can sign up to receive emails whenever Hayden Thorne publishes a new book. There's no charge and no obligation.

https://books2read.com/r/B-A-LFQC-FMYY

About the Author

I've lived most of my life in the San Francisco Bay Area though I wasn't born there (or, indeed, the USA). I'm married with no kids and three cats.

I started off as a writer of gay young adult fiction, specializing in contemporary fantasy, historical fantasy, and historical genres. My books ranged from a superhero fantasy series to reworked and original folktales to Victorian ghost fiction.

I've since expanded to gay New Adult fiction, which reflects similar themes as my YA books and varies considerably in terms of romantic and sexual content.

While I've published with a small press in the past, I now self-publish my books. Please visit my site for exclusive sales and publishing updates.

Read more at https://haydenthorne.com.